CHASING DUST CLOUDS

DUSTY LOVE SERIES
BOOK 1

LILLIANA ROSE

Chasing Dust Clouds

By Lilliana Rose

Copyright 2015 Lilliana Rose

ISBN-13: 9780987213365

To my sister, Annette,
keep on farming on.

INFORMATION AND DICTIONARY

This book has been written using US English, but the book's story is set in Australia. Some euphemisms that form part of the Australian spoken word may be used. If you would like further explanation, or to discuss Australia, please do not hesitate to contact the author. Contact details have been provided, for your convenience, at the end of this book.

Akubra – Felt hat traditionally worn by farmers

Anzac – Australian and New Zealand Army Corps.

Ballsed it up – An activity done very badly, making mistakes.

Bloody – A swear word used to emphasize a comment or angry statement.

Bugger off – To leave or go away, rude way of telling someone to leave.

Bush – Refers to sparsely settled areas of Australia, usually scrub-covered or forested wilderness.

Chuffed – Ppleased with yourself.

Cuppa – A cup of tea.

Good drop – Usually refers to wine.

Hard Yakka – Australian workwear including shoes

Jackaroo or jackarooing – A young man living and working on a sheep or cattle station.

Jubilee cake – A light fruit cake.

Mate – Refers to a friend.

Mob – A group of sheep also known as a flock or herd.

Mud map – A map drawn roughly as a set of directions.

Nick – To steal.

Oi – Used to attract someone's attention.

Op shop – A store that sells used clothing and household items.

Pear-shaped – Situation that's gone awry, perhaps horribly wrong.

Pub – Hotel.

Quick smart – In a hurry.

Royal Adelaide Show – Annual agricultural show in Adelaide South Australia.

Sav blanc – Shortened name for Sauvignon Blanc wine which originates from the Bordeaux region of France.

Scones – A scone is a basic component of the

Devonshire tea. Lightly sweetened and dense it is served with butter or jam and cream.

Smoko – Aa short break from work.

Toff – Derogatory stereotype for someone who acts rich or an upper-class person.

Ute – A utility vehicle or pick-up.

Vegemite – A thick black spread made from brewers' yeast and various vegetable and spice additives.

CHAPTER 1

"Gɪт ʙᴀᴄᴋ 'ᴇʀᴇ," yelled Dusty. She rested her arm on the open window of the ute and leaned out. "Git 'ere."

The dogs were walking too close to the ewes. There was a five-kilometer walk ahead to Acacia Plains, and she didn't want the ewes or the dogs to become exhausted.

Dusty whistled. Molly, a short-haired border collie cross, looked back, her tongue hanging out her mouth. Molly returned back to the sheep, trotting alongside Ted, a purebred Kelpie.

"Come 'ere." Dusty stopped the ute and waited.

Molly turned away from the sheep and ran back toward her boss, tail between her legs and her head down.

"Up." The dogs jumped on the back of the ute. Dusty could hear them puffing hard. Molly stretched forward through the gap between rails behind the ute cabin, her saliva dripped on Dusty's bare arm.

"Thanks a lot." Molly stretched closer to her owner. Dusty sighed. "Good girl." She patted the dog on the head and scratched her behind the ears before putting the ute into first gear and moving slowly toward the sheep but also keeping her distance.

Dusty yawned and leaned back. This was the second mob she'd moved today in readiness for shearing tomorrow. She needed a rest, but there were still too many jobs to do before the shearers arrived—*pen sheep, put bags in shed, get the vaccines, needles, and oil machines.* Then there were the daily jobs—*feed dogs, collect eggs, water the geese...*

An electronic bleat disrupted her thoughts. She picked up her phone from the dashboard to see the message.

Ho at you grand?

Dusty smiled as she tried to decode the message from her mom. *Maybe I should turn off the predictive text on Mom's phone?*

Her mom worried too much when she was working out on the farm alone. She couldn't blame her because of how her dad died three years ago. He had a heart attack while checking sheep, and it had taken all afternoon to find him. Then, at twenty-five, Dusty stepped up to work on the farm, something she always wanted to do, while her younger sister, Jody, went back to the city, and her mom developed a whole new level of worrying.

Dusty typed out a quick reply.

All OK :)

The dogs paced eagerly on the back of the ute, rocking the vehicle. Dusty looked ahead. The sheep walked around a bend in the road. In their eagerness to work, the dogs jumped off the ute and sprinted down the road racing each other to the sheep.

"Come back." They ignored her, and she hit the steering wheel in frustration. They were trained by her dad and only listened to him. They hadn't forgotten their old master. She put the phone on the dash. Dusty increased the speed of the ute to catch up and took the bend in the road.

A dust cloud rose up ahead.

"Great."

A car was coming. The last thing she needed was a scattered mob to regroup and get back to the farm before it got too dark. Rain, hail, or shine, shearing was going to start tomorrow and keep going until all fifteen hundred ewes were shorn.

The silver sports car came into sight over the small hill ahead. Dusty revved the ute, scaring the sheep enough so they pushed over to the left side of the road.

But there still wasn't enough room on the right side of the road for the car to pass.

"Come on."

The dogs helped the mob begin to stretch out a little, and the space on the road widened. Dusty tooted the horn to hurry the ewes along.

The silver car kept coming toward her.

"Slow down." Dusty's knuckles turned white as she gripped the steering wheel tighter. The car didn't look familiar, besides no one around here drove a silver sports car with a convertible roof. The car moved to the side where she'd directed the sheep.

"Idiot. All you have to do is wait." Her heart thudded with panic.

The car's speed reduced. But it wasn't enough. It kept driving straight toward the sheep. The sheep didn't know what to do. Even the dogs were confused and jumped on the back of the ute.

"Shit." She quickly wound down the window and put her hand out signaling the driver to stop.

The car kept coming.

Dusty had no choice but to stop. She motioned again for the other driver to stop.

"Stop, *stop*, STOP," she yelled even though there was no way she would've been heard.

The sheep hesitated. One ewe looked at the road ahead and bolted. The others followed.

"Phew." Dusty stared at the car unimpressed. She

saw the four joined rings in the front of the car. *Who would drive such a posh car out here?*

The Audi driver tooted his horn. The sudden noise spooked the ewes, and they scattered in all directions.

"Shit." Some of the ewes collided with each other. "Stop!"

The car kept moving forward.

Dusty knew what was going to happen.

She closed her eyes.

She didn't want to see.

The thud caused an angry fire to flare within her. Dusty got out of the ute and ran over to the lump of wool lying on the road. She knelt down. The ewe was still breathing but she had two broken legs.

"Oh my God, my God." A man in a light gray suit came running toward her. A clean aroma wafted around, and she could smell his spicy aftershave as he stopped next to her.

Dusty stood up. "You fuckin' idiot. Why couldn't you slow down?"

"I'm sorry. I just didn't know what to do."

"So why couldn't you fuckin' stop then?" Something inside of her snapped. Her anger flooded out. She clenched her hands to help keep herself under control.

"It's still breathing."

The man stood near the sheep. He ran his hand through his dark hair, looked to the sky, then the sheep and put his hand on his forehead. "Oh my God."

"No thanks to you. How hard was it to stop?" She wasn't going to make it easy for this loser. He'd just killed one of her ewes.

"I... I... dunno. I thought they'd just get out of the way." He looked at the sheep.

"Driving that fast?" Dusty glared at him. "You thought they'd sprint like a fuckin' tiger and get out of your way." She didn't usually swear, but this man had boiled her over. She re-clenched her fists.

"Sorry. I didn't mean it. Oh my God." He looked pale, and his hand trembled as he ran it through his hair again. "I don't like to harm anything."

"Well, you did."

"At least it's still breathing."

"Not for much longer."

His eyes widened. "I'll pay for a vet. It will be fine." He took out his phone. "What's the number?"

"The best thing is for her to be put out of her misery."

"No, no, no. I can afford a vet. The cost won't be a problem."

Dusty's heat turned to white hot. "I can see that."

"I'm sorry." He held up the phone trying to see the screen in the sunlight. "A vet will have her walking soon enough. I'll pay."

"It will never be enough," said Dusty. The potential loss cut at her heart. The what ifs piled into her mind. It was one of her better breeding ewes, the future of her farm.

"It's only a sheep."

Dusty clenched her hands closed so her nails dug into her skin. "It's a ewe. A pregnant ewe," said Dusty. *A ewe that had been bred by my dad.* She took a deep breath.

"I'm *really* sorry. I'm not used to driving out here." His forehead wrinkled with sincerity.

"No shit. The sire of this unborn lamb cost three grand."

"Shit, for a sheep?" His dark eyebrows raised in disbelief.

"Let's not forget, you just killed his son or daughter as well as the mother." She narrowed her eyes at him, keeping her hands by her side. God, she wanted to hit him.

"It was an accident."

"Not the fuckin' way you drove."

"You shouldn't have your sheep on the bloody road."

His words flamed her anger. "Idiots like you shouldn't be driving."

"Plenty of paddock space here. Roads are for cars not sheep."

Her anger spilled over. "Look around. This is farming country. Sheep are moved on the road, and fuckheads like you stay in the city." She looked him square in the eyes not giving in.

He lowered his eyes. "What do you want, name your price?"

His words hit her like rocks. Dusty turned away as her eyes went hot and swelled with tears. *What do I want?* "Turn back time and not run over the fuckin' sheep in the first place."

This wasn't about money. He'd killed a sheep bred by her dad, and old grief flooded through her body. There was nothing he could do to make it right. *Nothing.* Her anger simmered. "Help me get her on the back of the ute."

"You'll take her to the vet?"

Dusty glared at him. "You don't fuckin' get it, do ya?" She walked over to the driver's side of the ute and reached behind the seat pulling out the rifle. "No need to take her to the vet for a job I can do."

"Bloody hell, woman," said the man. "You don't need to be doing that."

Dusty turned to look at him. He had a broad jawline, thick soft hair, and nice eyes, the sort of eyes you wouldn't mind staring at for hours. He appeared fit and strong, and his expensive suit looked absolutely great on him. She wasn't used to looking at men who were so dressed up and sexy. Dusty's mouth went dry. In different circumstances, there might have been something between them. She took a deep breath to focus. *No way. Not now.*

Dusty loaded the gun.

"Really, come on, you don't have to do this."

"It's cruel to keep her alive," answered Dusty. She steeled herself against the job she had to do. Grief cut away at her stomach as she walked up to the ewe on the ground.

"Please—"

Dusty glared at him. "What? You want to do this for me, do you?"

His face paled. He froze, staring at her with big blue innocent eyes.

"That's what I thought."

She faced the ewe, raised the gun, aimed, and fired.

The sound of the gun vibrated through her body, slicing away at her flesh. One shot was enough, blood oozed out from the wound and onto the dry dirt. The ewe was out of her misery now, but instead, a whole lot of misery pulsed within Dusty as she returned the rifle behind the seat. Her knees wobbled and her head felt light. *At least it's no longer suffering.*

She glared at the city boy, who stood there, mouth gaping open in shock, his face pale and shoulders slumped forward. *Yeah, welcome to the country.* A lump in her throat stopped her from speaking out loud.

Dusty took a deep breath. There was work to be done. She gripped the legs of the dead ewe tightly to stop her hands from shaking. "Grab the back legs."

"But I'll get dirty." He just stood there immobile as if she had pointed the rifle at him. "Do you know how much this suit cost?"

"Good to hear you're supporting the wool industry. Now be a man and grab her back legs."

He swallowed hard and hesitated.

"You said you'd do anything," said Dusty.

He came over and took hold of the back legs. He barely strained under the weight of the woolly ewe. *Gym junkie, it fits with the car and the suit.* "Swing her onto the back on three... one... two... three."

The ewe landed on the back of the ute with a thud, and he winced.

"Poor thing."

He held his hands out not sure what to do with them. They were covered in dirt and there was a brown smear on his trousers.

Good, thought Dusty. Frustration burned through her veins. *It's what he deserves.*

"You're strong," he said.

He took out his black leather wallet and pulled out a handful of fifties and hundreds. "Here, I know it's not enough, but I can send more later."

"You don't get it, do you?" Dusty didn't have the energy to be angry anymore. It was done, and she had to get the mob back together and focus on shearing. Not thinking about a good-looking man who rocked her world on so many levels.

He stood holding out the money. "No."

"Just go back to your posh car and get the fuck out of here." She put her hands on her hips and glared at him.

He paused then shoved the money in his wallet and walked to his car. He turned back as he opened the door. "I'm sorry." Then he got into his car.

"Good riddance." She put her hand on the ewe's head while tears slid down her face.

CHAPTER 2

BLAISE SHUT the car door and held his breath. *What's that god-awful smell?* It was rotten and stinky like shit. The stench reflected how he felt like crap for running over her sheep. *She killed it right there and then.* He glanced through the windshield at her. She looked exhausted, angry, and ready to bring out the rifle to use it on him. He looked away. Something else stirred inside of him.

He turned the key in the ignition taking shallow breaths to avoid the smell. Something about the woman caught his attention. His heart pounded fast causing pain in his chest. Her image burned in his mind. Her light brown hair was messed up with bits of sticks in it. A dirt mark on one of her high cheekbones, her shapely hips, and a sassy attitude screamed at him to take action. *I can't now.*

His hands shook, and he gripped the steering

wheel tight. He'd never hit a living thing before, and he'd never seen anyone like her. She certainly wasn't like the city women he was used to.

Blaise took a deep breath and gagged from the smell. He knew she was waiting for him to go, and he knew he was expected to do this quickly. But he couldn't. He wanted to get back out of the car to reason with her, make her understand he was truly sorry, and as cliché as the saying was, he'd turn back time and slow down for God's sake.

The memory of the glare she'd given him when he said 'sorry' stopped him. Her blue eyes were still burning through him. He knew he was beat.

"In three hundred meters, turn right." The GPS brought him back to reality. He crunched into first gear and drove away. There wasn't anything else he could do. *Best to get out of here.*

"... in one hundred meters turn right."

Blaise looked back at her through the rearview mirror. He couldn't see her face. A cloud of dust rose up behind him concealing his last chance to see her. He wanted to go back. Instead, he kept driving.

She didn't even cry. She was a mystery, one he wanted to solve over a candlelight dinner and a bottle of red. But that was absurd. He'd blown his chance before even meeting her. It wouldn't work. There was no way she'd let him close enough to just talk together.

Put her out of your mind, he told himself. *Better that way. A tough chick like her would only bust your balls all the time*. And he'd had enough of ball-breaking women.

Besides, dickhead, you just killed her sheep. His gut churned. Stomach acid rose like a volcanic eruption. He hit the brakes hard. The car slid to an abrupt stop. He opened the door just in time as he spewed his lunch onto the dirt road.

Blaise wiped his mouth. A fly landed on his nose, and he swatted it away as more flies came into the car and buzzed around him.

He paused. There was something else he hadn't realized. The silence. It chilled him and caused his skin to prickle. There was no sound of cars or people talking. He quickly closed the door, shutting out the quiet he wasn't used to.

Blaise leaned over and turned on the CD player. 'The Ring' Opera music clashed and banged as the music which always reminded him of Bugs Bunny being hunted, vibrated in his car, pushing the silence from his mind.

"That's better." He glanced down to put the car in gear and noticed his trousers. *Damn it*. There was a smear of something brown along his thigh. *Just bloody fuckin' great*. He wasn't sure how the hell he was meant to impress a client now, or how to explain how he got shit on his trousers without mentioning he'd run over a sheep.

He drove down the road, trying to keep his attention on finding Aaron Jackson's farm, his first client visit in the country. The least he could do now was to try and turn up on time, and the chance of that was diminishing rapidly.

His boss, Danny Palmer, sent him out to the country to visit clients to do their taxes this year, a change for them, so they didn't have to come to the city. It had been a tough year financially, and his boss thought this would be a nice gesture to the country clients. Danny also made it clear he was looking for a junior partner in his business. Blaise knew he couldn't say no. At twenty-eight, a junior partner would be a great mark of how successful he was at his work. He thought a week in the country would do him good— change of scenery, fresh air, and all that. How wrong had he been? Today was the worst Monday he'd ever experienced.

His mates also thought it would be great for him to go to the country. They reckoned it would be the best way for him to meet a woman.

Yeah, they were bloody wrong. He'd been warned about how fast gossip traveled out here, and he figured he'd be known as a sheep killer and no one would want to know him. He swallowed hard. His throat burned from the aftertaste of bile.

"Turn around."

"Damn it." He slowed down and did a U-turn, which ended up in about a five-point turn on the narrow road. He hadn't seen the road he was meant to have taken. Blaise over-accelerated and stones flung into the air as the wheels spun. He eased off the accelerator not wanting to chip the paintwork of his car. *I should've hired a ute or something.*

"... turn right."

Blaise looked in the direction he was meant to take and saw a rusty sign. The paint was peeling off, and it was difficult to read.

RB&MA Jackson and Sons. An outline of a sheep and a sheaf of wheat were painted under the name.

Scrub lined the driveway, and then there were flat paddocks for as far as he could see. *Brown, so much brown*. He hadn't realized there were so many shades of brown. He could see how this sort of area would be the ideal setting for a sci-fi movie set on a barren moon.

The driveway opened out to a large area, sheds on the left, not the sort of sheds he was used to seeing in the city. These sheds were bigger than most houses he'd lived in. He let out a long whistle.

Nearby dust bellowed from sheep running around between pens. He saw a guy who looked about the same age as him and assumed he was Aaron. Blaise couldn't make any sense of the direction the sheep were running in and where they were meant to be going. The last thing he wanted to do was to get close to a sheep again, so he looked around for some shade to park.

Blaise pulled up the hand brake, turned off the car, and got out. The heat hit him just as hard as the acidic smell of sheep. A horde of flies came out of nowhere and began annoying him. He was about to shrug out his jacket, that's what he would've done in the city. Out here he realized how unnecessary that was. Besides, his trousers were already ruined.

"G'day," said Aaron sauntering over. He held out his hand. "Aaron."

"Blaise." They shook hands.

"Found the place all right, then?" Aaron wore an Akubra hat, dusted and aged, blue shirt, blue jeans, and was completely covered in dust.

Blaise felt overdressed for the occasion. He was beginning to wonder if a junior partnership was worth this experience. *Of course, it is.* Partnership in the business was what he wanted before he even finished his uni degree and got a job. It was all part of his plan, a small step toward running his own business. "Yes, GPS is a great invention."

"Don't trust 'em much myself."

One of the dogs jumped on Blaise. He patted the dog trying not to think if the dog's claws ripped his expensive suit trousers.

"Get down," grumbled Aaron to the dog.

Blaise gave the dog a quick rub behind the ears. Satisfied, the dog jumped down and ran off to lay down in the shade. Blaise was going to have a serious word with his boss when he got back. *He should've warned me about what it was like out here in the sticks and told me to wear more casual clothes.*

"Sorry about that," said Aaron. "Looks like the dog messed up your pants."

Blaise looked down at his suit trousers. The mark had been there before, but he wasn't about to say that. "Don't worry about it."

"If you say so." Aaron began walking toward the house. "Come inside, Ma will have afternoon tea for us."

"Thanks." Blaise got his satchel, full of the accounting documents he needed, from the back of the car. He locked his car.

"No need to lock ya car out here. Dog's not going to nick it."

"Of course." Blaise wasn't used to this. Usually, he was the one in charge. The one making comments. The one dishing out instructions.

He followed Aaron inside. He knew he had his work cut out for him if he wanted to gain any sort of respect from these people. All he could think was that he'd killed a sheep, and the owner was someone he wanted to get to know. He had a lot of ground to catch up, and so far, he was still back- peddling.

CHAPTER 3

THE MOB WAS SPLIT. Sheep were ahead of her, behind her, and she had a bad feeling some even managed to go down the track further up which was going to be difficult to get them back in the ute. A motorbike or horse would make it easier, but she didn't have either. She was going to be lucky to get the mob home before dark.

Dusty kicked her boots into the ground as she walked along the road looking into the scrub for renegade ewes. That stranger, in his sexy car and smart suit, came along at the wrong time. Dusty knew she shouldn't be thinking about him at all, but his image kept coming to mind with his dark hair and strong, carved facial features.

She reminded herself of what he did. *Stupid idea falling for a city boy, especially one who can't drive for shit.*

There was only one option left. She had to ask for

help. Aaron was the last person she wanted to ask. She wiped her eyes with the corner of her sleeve. *Aaron. Her ex.* The one she'd shut out of her life because her dad died, and she wanted to run the farm, not have her future husband wrestling in on her territory. It always complicated things when she asked him for help.

Dusty looked down the road. About half the mob was missing. On days like this, she wished she'd given up the country life for the city, like her younger sister. The longest she'd spent in the city was each year at the Royal Adelaide Show for about five days. That was way too long to be in a city surrounded by concrete, lights, and too many people. The wide-open spaces called to her. She knew this was the life she wanted. It was more than in her blood, it was in her bones, and it was who she was. Her identity. She wouldn't give this life up for anyone.

Dusty took out her phone and wiped a layer of dust from the screen. She bought up Aaron's details. *Text or phone?* She didn't want to speak to him, which was stupid because if he turned up to help, she'd have to speak to him. Besides, he agreed to help her tomorrow in the shed, so she'd have to talk to him then. Over the last few years, he'd been there for her, yet she still didn't want to go back to having an intimate relationship with him. There was nothing remotely romantic between them, it was deeper than that, but she couldn't quite figure it out. Things weren't peaceful between them, and her stomach knotted uncomfortably whenever she thought of him.

The pressure was getting too much. *Who else to ask?*

Her mom would come down in a flash, but she didn't want to ask her. Her mom had recovered successfully from a hip replacement six months ago. Chasing sheep in scrub, on dirt roads full of loose stones wasn't going to be good for her new hip. It felt wrong to ask Aaron, but she used the touch screen to call him. *He's a neighbor. It's the neighborly thing to do to come and help out, nothing more than that.*

The phone rang three times before he picked up.

"Hello, Dusty. How can I help you?"

"You don't know I want your help," she answered defensively. His voice fueled old anger inside of her.

"You do need my help, though, don't you?"

Dusty chewed on her bottom lip. Then sighed. She'd come this far. "I'm having trouble moving the mob of sheep some idiot came through and scattered. Can you come over and help me?"

"Sure, where are ya?"

Dusty's eyes watered with relief. This still didn't feel right to be asking Aaron, and she was sure she'd regret it, but the hope of him coming to help eased her stress. "About three K's south of the farm. Can you come on your bike?"

"Sure. I'll be there in about twenty."

Dusty hung up and shoved the phone in her pocket and wiped her eyes. At least he'd help her, and the sheep will be penned at the shearing shed ready for tomorrow. That was all that mattered to her right now.

∼

"HEY MATE, I've gotta go help out a neighbor," said Aaron. He sat back down at the nineteen-sixty style kitchen table.

"That's fine," said Blaise. They only managed to get through about half of the accounts that needed to be discussed because of the interjections about farm life.

Blaise rubbed his temples. He knew way too much about the life cycle of sheep and how to read the weather by looking at the clouds. He needed some strong coffee made from a café machine, not the instant he'd been drinking.

"We can do the rest later." Blaise certainly didn't need any more food. Mrs. Jackson had been over-generous with homemade cakes and slices. *I'm going to have to find out if there's a local gym.*

"You don't know anything about scattering a mob of sheep?" asked Aaron.

Blaise gulped and nearly choked.

"You met Dusty then."

Blaise tried to hide his face with the mug and took another sip of instant coffee. He just knew the incident this afternoon was going to haunt him for a long time, and haunt in a bloodsucking-zombie kind of way, not like an innocent, transparent-ghost way.

Aaron's laugh was like claws scratching along his back.

"Don't worry about it. I'll go and clean up your mess. Maybe I'll come into town tonight, get you meeting some of the locals, so you're not bored this week. Then we can finish the accounts in a more civilized way over a cold beer or two."

"Sure." If it meant he didn't have to drive down county roads, then he'd happily meet Aaron at the pub. "I go back to Adelaide Friday afternoon." He shuffled the papers back into a neat pile and dusted off some crumbs from the Jubilee cake he'd been eating.

"In a hurry to get back to the city lights? Or you got a girl that's wanting attention?" Aaron pushed the chair back, the metal legs scrapped on the linoleum floor as he got up.

Blaise wished he had a girl to hurry back to. He liked the idea of that. But what he really wanted was to go back home and gain some control back in his life. To go out and have drinks with his mates and have the same old conversations about buying real estate, sci-fi movies, horror stories, and girls, not sheep, rain, and grain. "What's the quickest way back to town?"

"Go out the driveway, turn left and keeping going until you get to the bitumen. Then turn right, and you'll go straight into town." Aaron grinned cheekily.

Blaise doubted it would be that easy. There were so many un-named roads around here going in all directions. He remembered one intersection he'd passed on the way had five roads converging together. In the end, he'd picked the one on the left. Luckily, it had been the correct road, but then not long after that he'd run over the sheep and met Dusty.

"I'll draw him a mud map," said Mrs. Jackson. She rummaged around in a kitchen drawer and took out an old envelope and pencil and began drawing.

"Thanks," said Blaise. He filed the papers away in his satchel and stood up.

"Here's the map." Mrs. Jackson handed over an empty envelope which had the hand-drawn map on the back.

"This is where you're now and here's Wilkton. Just follow the thicker line."

"Thanks." It wasn't quite a simple turn left and go straight ahead. He was going to have to be a little more on guard with Aaron and his 'country humor.' He was used to a bit of tussling for the top- dog position with the boys, but not like this. He looked at Aaron to let him know that he was on to him, but Aaron was already at the back door.

"Where are you staying?" asked Mrs. Jackson.

"At the pub."

"There's three of them in town, which one?"

"Ol' Billies, I think." He couldn't believe that such a small town would have three pubs. *Pub crawls must be hardcore.*

"Matilda's Waterhole, on the outskirts of town would be quieter," said Mrs. Jackson.

"I'll check it out."

"Make sure you do. It's much better than staying at the pub, and Mrs. Shorn will take good care of you."

"Thanks for the food," said Blaise.

"Wait, you should take the rest of the cake with you."

"No… that's fine—" Before he could finish, she had the cake in a Tupperware container and was handing it to him. "Thanks."

"Got to look after our city visitors." She smiled.

"Thanks. It's the best cake I've tasted."

Mrs. Jackson blushed and stood proudly.

If this is the welcome I get every time, then I'm in for a big week of eating.

Blaise walked out the back door of the home behind Aaron, clutching the container and mud map.

Outside, Aaron slipped on his work boots. Blaise braced himself as the dogs came up to greet him once more.

"Git down," grumbled Aaron as he stamped his feet.

The dogs backed off a little. Blaise didn't think his suit could tolerate much more of this country life.

"I'll catch you later tonight at the Ol' Billies pub," said Aaron.

"Sure." They shook hands.

Aaron whistled, and the dogs rushed ahead of him.

Blaise left out a long sigh and walked to his car. *So*

much for an easy week in the country. He was beat, stank, and had a pile of accounts still to sort through.

Blaise wrinkled his nose. A new rank smell wafted around him. He checked the bottom of his shoes, which were dusty and had a few stones caught in the grip. He looked around and then saw the source—wet marks on each of his tires from the dogs.

"Great." He opened the boot and put the cake and satchel inside. "Just bloody great."

CHAPTER 4

Aaron swung the chain around the metal post, closing the gate. "There you go, darlings. Sleep tight tonight."

Dusty's smile released some of the tension stored in her facial muscles. It had been a tough day, but with Aaron's help, they'd gotten the sheep back to Acacia Plains. They'd worked in the fading light as they struggled to get the last of the sheep into the yards around the shearing shed. If Aaron hadn't been cool, calm, and collected, she would've lost it. It was dark now, and she was indebted to him, and she knew he was going to enjoy the advantage.

The dogs ran up to Aaron for a pat. The ultimate betrayal for Dusty, but then they ran to her. She patted them. "You dogs worked all right."

"Hey, what about me?" asked Aaron as he walked over.

"Kneel down then." Dusty was relaxing somewhat, and her anger and trepidation toward Aaron had faded. He'd been all right to be around while they worked, his humor had been a welcome distraction.

Aaron knelt down in front of Dusty and tilted his head.

Dusty pinched his ear.

"Oww." He pulled back and rubbed his ear. "That wasn't part of the deal."

Dusty laughed. "Come and get some dinner. Mom would've cooked extra for you."

"Not so quick. I haven't had my ear rub."

Aaron grabbed her around the waist. Dusty squealed and tried to wriggle out of his grasp, but she wasn't quick enough.

Aaron pulled her backward, and she lost her balance toppling on top of him. He kept his grip on his prize so she couldn't escape. Aaron grinned cheekily, presenting his ear for a rub.

"Okay. Okay." Dusty decided to be gentler this time and ran the tip of her finger slowly from the side of his face to behind his ear, and then she circled her finger around his ear. He groaned and stretched his hands up her back, lifting himself up. In the light from the ute, his brown eyes were afire with her image. He kissed her before she had time to refuse.

"Aaron." This wasn't what she wanted.

They had their time trying to form a relation-ship. It hadn't worked out, and she didn't want to revisit this with him, about them as a couple. Despite them both being farmers, they didn't fit well together. There was just something about him. A twist in her gut warned her this wasn't right for her.

Aaron was known for his hot temper, which was easy to forget at times like this with his hands around her waist, his sweaty masculine scent, and the chance for her to lighten the physical work by having a man at her side. Her gut churned.

Not this man, she reminded herself.

She was going to trust her inner feeling. Something wasn't right between her and Aaron.

He kissed her again. It was hard to pull away from him. His lips soft against hers were the opposite of the roughness in his working hands, and she liked the contrast. He stroked her back. His touch made her feel safe and protected, but her insides knotted.

"Dusty." He brushed his lips over hers.

She shivered with desire and reached deep inside to find the resolve she needed to stop this. She pushed him back, but he pressed against her.

"No, Aaron. I won't." Her voice was strong and commanding.

Aaron kept his hold on her.

Dusty's heart pounded faster to a new rhythm, one that was erratic. She pushed him back, stronger this time, as she struggled to hold the panic which was slowly rising inside of her.

He gave in and moved away, releasing his grip. "We most certainly can."

"No. Not tonight."

His hands dropped down along her waist, tracing the outline of her figure. "Later then?"

She struggled to keep connected to her inner strength. Around here, he was quite the catch. Guilt gripped her throat and a pressure began to build. *No.* The tension eased. There was something about him that didn't match her. Something she didn't want to see, something hidden in his good deeds. She stood up. Aaron sighed in disappointment.

"Dinner?" She held out her hand to him to help him up. Maybe this was making things worse, having him around even if she didn't want anything intimate from him. She was going to have to come up with an alternative plan, employ one of the young farming lads, or figure out who else to ask for help.

"Okay, I'll cut my losses." He took her hand and pulled her tight to get up.

She struggled to keep her balance, especially when he was now standing face to face with her.

"But only if it's a dinner for two."

He brushed his body against hers. Instead of her skin prickling, her senses sharpened.

Dusty stepped back and began walking to the ute. Not now, not after the crap day she'd just had. She felt his gaze on her back as she walked, and the uneasy sensation returned to her gut. "Mom would've cooked more than enough for the three of us." Her mom loved to cook, and she'd begun preparing the shearers' meals for the next four days, so there would be plenty of food.

Dusty got behind the wheel. She whistled, and the dogs jumped on the back of the ute.

"What's gotten into you?" Aaron followed close behind.

"Nothing." She drove the ute to the back of the house. It was already late, nine o'clock. She should've rung her mom to warn her that she'd be coming in for dinner. Luckily, her mom was used to this. The sheep didn't always do what you wanted them to, machines broke down, and generally jobs seemed to take much longer on the farm.

Dusty stopped by the back gate. "I'll feed the dogs. Meet you inside." She wanted some space away from him to collect her thoughts. She was suddenly aware of what this could look like to her mom. While her mom always gave her space when it came to guys, there was no expectation. Besides, she was only twenty-eight, and she didn't want to be giving her mom the wrong idea. This was purely business. Aaron was a neighbor helping out. Her mom would get that, but it was just that they had a prior relationship, which complicated things. It had been a while since she dated. It made it harder to say no, even to Aaron when it wasn't feeling right. Being exhausted wasn't helping her keep a clear head either.

Deep in thought, she walked down toward the dog kennels in the dark. She'd grown up here and didn't need a torch. The night was clear so there was plenty of moonlight.

Dusty put her shoulder to the wooden door of the old dairy. It didn't budge.

"Here, let me." Aaron gently, but firmly, pushed her aside.

"I can do it." Dusty clenched her jaw tight. She hadn't realized he'd followed her.

"Sure you can, but I can help." He barely needed to push at the door before it opened. "Where's the light?"

"Don't need it. Here, get out of the way." She didn't want to be further indebted to him than she already was. She bustled past him with more force than she needed, and Aaron stumbled back into the old cupboard.

"Oww."

She ignored him and went over to the forty-pound bag of dog pellets as her eyes adjusted to the dark in the small back room of the old dairy. It stored bags of grain for the chooks, bags of pellets for the dogs, and a few pulleys, chains, and hooks for when her dad had butchered sheep.

She filled a tin with pellets. She wasn't comfortable with Aaron hanging around like a blowfly.

"Who knows what I'm going to catch in the dark," said Aaron as he walked toward Dusty. His hands found her waist and slipped around her tight. "Gotcha."

A sinister shiver ran down Dusty's back as his hot breath flowed over her skin. Her body switched gears into full alert. This wasn't what she wanted, and she'd let him know this. Her temperature began to rise. A bonfire glowed again inside of her.

"Hands off." She kept still in his embrace, not wanting to encourage his behavior.

"But..." He held her tight, his hands low below her waist. He pressed his lips into her neck, nibbling playfully.

"Let me go." She pushed away his hands, but he tightened his grip. Her heart pounded against her chest like the flames of a trapped fired gasping for oxygen.

"Come on, Dusty, we're made for each other." He nuzzled into her neck. "You love me, remember?"

The flames erupted inside of her and burned red hot. Dusty elbowed him, hard, in his ribs. She dropped the tin of dog pellets, and they scattered on the concrete floor.

"Shit." He pulled away in pain. But she wasn't finished, not now, as she unleashed her flames creating her own version of a bush fire. She could see well enough in the dark gray light. She punched him, right hook, collecting his cheek with her knuckles.

He reeled backward. "Fuck." He slapped her. Her

head snapped to the right. Dusty stumbled backward. He grabbed her wrists.

She tried to wrestle out of his grip, but he held her tight so she spat at him.

Surprised by her action, he released her.

"That all you got left in you?" He smirked.

"Next one's a kick." She tensed her leg muscles ready, focussed on fighting back, even though he was easily much stronger than her. She wasn't about to let him get away treating her like this. She remembered now, this darker side of Aaron, but he'd never threatened her physically like this before. Had he?

This was why she'd left.

The memory surfaced.

He'd been rough before.

"Unless you haven't got the message yet, I'm not interested in you."

"You wouldn't dare." He stepped in close to her.

She pulled back quickly giving herself enough space. Then kicked her steel-capped boot low into his shin. He groaned with pain.

"You want another one?"

He paused, the whites of his eyes flashed in the dark. "No man would want a bitch like you," he said while he limped to the door.

"Good." Her knees trembled.

"You fuckin' bitch." He paused at the door and looked back. Molly and Ted growled at him, baring their teeth. "You can fuckin' do your own work tomorrow in the shed. I won't be fuckin' helping a fuckin' bitch like you."

"Good, I don't want a man like you around anyway." She surprised herself how steady her voice sounded while her body shook uncontrollably in the darkness of the shed.

"Go fuck yourself." He turned away. "Git out of it," he growled at the dogs.

They snapped back at him as he walked away.

Dusty sunk to her knees on the cold, dirty concrete floor. *Shit. What am I going to do now?* She couldn't get another shed hand for shearing at such late notice.

Dusty leaned forward trying to pick up the spilled pellets, but her hands trembled too much. Her knuckles hurt. She forced her fingers to move against the pain. She heard Aaron's motorbike.

Molly came up to Dusty, whining with concern.

"I'm okay, old girl. We don't need him."

Ted pushed her nose into Dusty's hand, ignoring the food, and licked her palm.

Aaron had never behaved this aggressive before. She'd always thought she could handle him, keep him sweet with her teasing and humor. *How stupid am I?*

"Dinner for two now tonight." This one was going to be harder to explain to her mom than Aaron actually turning up for dinner.

Ted licked her cheek reminding her of the stinging ache in her face, which intensified as her adrenaline levels dropped. "Bastard." Ted pushed himself into her in a doggy-style hug. Dusty buried her face in his thick coat, ignoring the prickles and dirt, finding the comfort in what was offered.

"We'll be okay." Dusty believed what she said. She had to since there was no way she was about to give up what she loved doing for a man or anyone else. "We'll be just fine." She squeezed her eyes shut tight and wrapped her arms around Ted. "We *will* be fine."

CHAPTER 5

Blaise skidded to a halt in front of the reception of Matilda's Waterhole as the last of the day's light faded. Mrs. Jackson had marked the place on the map she'd drawn, and he'd figured this was the place to stay. Finding the motel had been much harder than he expected.

The battery on his GPS went flat. He'd misplaced the cord and taken the wrong turn, many times. The darker it became, the more frustrated he was and the more his stomach grumbled. After stopping and asking for directions, three times, enduring laugher and negative comments about his sense of direction, his choice of car to drive on dirt roads, and even his dirty suit, he finally made it here.

The sign out the front of Matilda's Waterhole flashed 'NO Vacancies.' Blaise drove in any way wondering how on earth a place like this, in the middle of almost nowhere, could have no vacancies. He figured the sign must be wrong.

Blaise got out of the car, slammed the door shut, and walked through the dust he'd stirred up. All he wanted now was a shower, a change of clothes, and to get out of the heat and dust. And a beer, he wanted to enjoy a cold beer, a big steak, and then maybe another beer. He swatted at the flies as he walked to reception. They buzzed around his head, hundreds of them, making him feel dirty as if he hadn't showered for a week.

The sign in the window said closed. "Just my luck." He cupped his hands to look through the window to see if anyone was at the reception desk. No one was there. He went in anyway. Bells clanked on the glass section of the door.

"Just a moment," someone yelled from further inside the office.

Blaise walked to the desk and waited. A desk fan moved the hot air around the office. He amused himself by looking at the brochures in the rack by the desk. It didn't look like there were too many places to eat besides the three pubs. There was an Italian restaurant, Ciao, that did look a bit more upscale, and there was a fish and chip shop.

"Hello, dear, can I help you?" A woman stood up from behind the reception holding a mouse trap with a dead mouse dangling from it.

Blaise jumped back from the desk. The horror

movies he'd been watching flooded into his mind, and his heart pounded quicker.

"Sorry, the tail end of a mouse plague." She smiled. "Pardon the pun."

Blaise wasn't sure he wanted to stay here for the night. No matter how much he needed a shower and to dress in clean clothes, sharing a room with rodents was not on his list. "Umm... a room until Friday?"

"Didn't you see the sign? No vacancies. Has the bulb gone again? Damn Rod, I'll bloody put the broom to him if he doesn't fix things when I ask him."

Blaise stood staring at the women. *Oh yeah, I'm not in Kansas anymore.* All he wanted to do was to get back to Adelaide. This was too much for him to handle out here.

"A... a... room would be great, just the one, for a week."

"Well, do you have a booking?"

Blaise just kept staring at the mouse. Its tail swung as if it was still alive. "No."

"Well, now, that's going to be a problem." She narrowed her eyes. "Hang on a minute, are you that toff from the city?"

Blaise cringed. *What rumors have I managed to start?* "Maybe." *At least she didn't say sheep killer.*

Sweat ran down his back even though he'd left his suit jacket in the car. Out of desperation, he'd rolled up the long sleeves of his wrinkle-free shirt as the heat was also getting to him. Even though the sun had set, it was still damn hot.

"You just come from the Jacksons?"

"Yeah." Maybe his luck was sort of holding.

"Well, you took your bloody time getting here. Marjorie rang hours ago and booked you a room."

Thank God for Marjorie Jackson. "She did?"

"Yeah, the last one, you're one lucky man." She moved her hands around as she talked forgetting she was holding a dead mouse in a trap.

He stared at the mouse. Bile rose up from his stomach, and he swallowed hard. "Popular town then."

"We're not actually a bad tourist destination, even the mice think so." She laughed.

"Well, I'm sure I'll see a few of the sites during my week here. Do you do laundry?"

He didn't think he could put this suit back on again unless it had been cleaned.

"Nope. There's a laundromat in town, just off the main street. I'll just get rid of this mouse." She turned around and went out the door behind her. "Rod, where are ya? Go check that sign, will ya?"

Great. He could do his own laundry, but he didn't think his expensive suit would wash up well at a laundromat.

"What about dry cleaning?" he yelled after her.

He couldn't see her, and there was no reply. Blaise stood awkwardly at the counter wondering what do to next. The door opened behind him, and he turned to see an older man standing right in the middle of the doorway. "Hello. Is Beryl looking after you?"

Blaise wasn't so sure that the answer was a simple yes. "I guess so."

"Good, good. Right then, just don't say I was here."

"You better not be letting any flies inside, Rod," yelled Beryl from the back room.

Rod shut the door and rushed off as Beryl came back into the room. Blaise was relieved to see she no longer carried the dead mouse.

"Was that Rod? Where's he gone now? He'd better be doing those jobs I asked him to do."

Blaise swallowed, debating whether or not to answer. *Poor man.* He decided to keep quiet. He didn't want to lose the only room left, even if there were mice running around everywhere.

Beryl took out a clipboard and put it on the counter. "Just fill this out and then you can have your key, and I need a deposit."

Blaise took out his wallet, pulled out his credit card and handed it over to Beryl. He picked up the pen and started filling out his details.

"Drycleaners open at nine tomorrow morning. They're next to the laundromat. Can't miss it." She finally answered his question.

"Thanks. Can you recommend a place to eat?"

He wasn't sure how he was actually going to find it without instructions, but he didn't dare ask because you can't miss it, and he didn't want Beryl to use the broom on him. The women out here definitely had balls and they were tough. He felt rather prissy and weak in comparison. This was not what he was used to feeling at all.

"Well, the Italian place isn't half bad, bit pricey if you ask me, but I'm sure you'll be able to afford it."

Blaise cringed at the remark. *God they must think I'm loaded.*

"Or there's the pub, Ol' Billies. They serve up something half decent."

"Thanks." He wasn't dripping in money, but he did like buying things he liked. In the city, no one would look twice at him wearing his suit and driving his Audi, though they might if the shit stain couldn't be removed.

"You better hurry up and get there, don't dilly dally, they close early." She swiped his card.

Blaise handed the completed form to Beryl then typed in his pin.

"Hard to say, depends if they're busy. Since it's a Monday night, they probably won't be, so if you want some tucker, get into town quick smart when you're done here."

"Okay." He smiled as he handed back the completed form. She didn't smile back. Her face remained stern.

"Right, now that you're sorted, here's your key, number twenty-six, last room on the right at the end of the row." She held out the key. He noticed the key ring was an oversized sheep.

His throat constricted. He was going to have to get in contact with that woman again, Dusty, and right the wrong. His conscience wasn't going to let this go any time soon.

"I'll bring over breakfast at seven, can't leave it outside 'cause of the flies and mice, so make sure you're up to take it."

Blaise held onto the key tightly. Who would've thought a trip to the country would be so intimidating. "Thanks," he managed to squeak out.

He wasn't sure if he should request something for breakfast, or just shut up and accept whatever was bought to him. He swallowed his words. He'd made such a mess of things already, and he didn't want to create further waves or a tsunami. If he could manage to fly under the radar for the rest of the week, then that would be an improvement. A black op attitude was what was needed—get in, do the job, and get out. Otherwise, there was no hope of becoming a junior partner.

"Rod, where are ya?" Beryl turned and disappeared back into the office.

Blaise drove his car to room number twenty-six and parked out front. He took in a deep breath. It would be easy to turn around and drive back to Adelaide and tell his boss to come down here and do this himself. He could endure the teasing, it wouldn't last that long. Maybe he could get the partnership by working longer hours for the next three years, or however long it would take for Danny to forget about this mess he'd made in only one afternoon. *Yeah right*, he knew he wouldn't be satisfied if he left. He got out and went to the room door.

Blaise paused as he put the key in the lock. He really didn't know what to expect with this type of motel. *It can't be that bad if Marjorie booked me in here.* He turned the key and opened the door. He paused, half expecting a mouse to run out. One didn't, so he walked into the room.

It wasn't half bad, simple but clean, which was saying something considering there were mice, flies, and clouds of dust that blew aimlessly around here. Blaise couldn't help thinking he'd stepped back in time and found his own time machine. If only it worked for real, he'd be able to change the last few hours, and the meeting with Dusty would've led to dinner.

The room had a distinct seventies style with its brown carpet, worn, melamine furniture, a double bed, with a brown and maroon cover. The bed headboard and side tables were made of dark, fake wood melamine. It smelled of lavender cleaning fluid, which still didn't mask the musty smell or how bad he smelled.

It will do. He shut the door and flicked on the air conditioning. The pipes sighed as it started up. Blaise went straight for the shower, stripping his clothes off quickly, letting them drop to the floor. He breathed a sigh of relief under the cool water and allowed the events of the day to wash away. There was one thing he couldn't wash away from his mind—Dusty. He really did wish he could get to know her.

Get control of yourself, he thought to himself as he finished up in the shower.

He dried himself vigorously trying to get Dusty out of his mind, then he wrapped the hotel's white towel around this waist and walked into the main room.

Blaise sat on the bed and flopped back, exhausted. The mattress was firm as he liked it. He began to drift away to sleep that was until his stomach rumbled, and he remembered what Beryl had said. There was no way he could go without food tonight, even though he'd overeaten on cakes, his stomach wanted some dude food right now.

He looked at his expensive discarded suit on the floor, and knew he couldn't put it back on. Not until it was cleaned. Then he realized what he'd done. In his eagerness to get cleaned up, he left his suitcase and suit bag in his car.

"Dammit."

He got up and carefully moved the curtain aside and looked out. His car was the only car parked in front of the rooms, and no one else seemed to be around. Plus, it was now completely dark except for the few areas lit up by outside lights.

I'll be quick. He tightened the towel around this

waist, grabbed his keys, clicking the lock to open the boot from inside to give himself some extra time. He took a deep breath and strolled out as if this was a natural thing to be doing, grabbed the case and suit bag, and slammed the boot.

A wolf whistle, sharp and loud, made him freeze. "Shit."

He hadn't thought anyone was around.

"Ya game, mate."

Blaise looked around trying to see who had seen him. There was another row of rooms and scrub to the right, but he couldn't see anyone.

"Might be quiet out here, but do something like that, and ya can bet someone will see ya."

He saw Rod looking out from one of the rooms. "Ah... okay," said Blaise.

Goddamn, another mistake to add to my ever-increasing list.

He rushed inside but not quick enough. His towel fell from his waist just as he stepped inside the room. He heard another wolf whistle. His face flushed.

"I like the new scenery," yelled Beryl.

Blaise didn't look back. He slammed the door shut leaving the towel outside. *So much for keeping out of the spotlight.* He knew he'd just added a new vine for the gossipers to use.

He opened his suitcase. *What was I thinking?* He had his toilet bag, shaving gear, gym gear, and business notes, and that was it. In his suit bag he at least had another suit to wear tomorrow, four shirts and two ties. That wasn't what he wanted to wear down to the local pub tonight. He stared at his open suitcase willing the clothes to morph into something that he'd be comfortable wearing on the weekend.

"Why didn't I pack some casual T-shirts and jeans?" He took out his gym clothes. They were old, color faded, and smelled faintly of his sweat even though they were clean. The shorts were Lycra based and tight, if they were loose shorts then maybe he could get away wearing them to the pub.

I was hopeful. He assumed there would be a gym where he stayed. It was what he was used to. This was still his best option. Blaise put them on and went outside, flicking the towel back into the room before locking the door and sliding into the safety of this car.

On the way into town he couldn't help thinking of Dusty. *Maybe I'll see her at the pub?*

Blaise was torn. It would be good to see her, but then it wasn't likely she'd be happy to see him.

If only I had slowed down, I might have had a date tonight instead.

He found Ol' Billies without any trouble, parked and walked to the hotel. *Damn.* Blaise got out of the car. He'd left Aaron's accounts back in the motel. He took a deep breath. *Guess that will have to wait.*

Blaise walked to the pub with too many thoughts he'd rather not think about—Dusty, the increasing workload, and killing a sheep.

Blaise pushed on the pub door and stepped inside. Everyone turned to look at him. Blaise wished he'd decided to wear his suit. *Mistake number fifty-nine.* He squared his shoulders refusing to be intimidated and walked up to the bar. *Best to make the most of this.*

The waitress smiled at him. A big smile, like she knew something about him. *I'm being paranoid.* He took a deep breath.

"What would you like?" she asked.

He scanned the menu board. "Steak, medium rare, thanks."

"The mushroom sauce is to die for."

Blaise read her name badge, Kate.

"Thanks."

It was like the room had gone dark, and there was a spotlight on him. Everyone was giving him the once over, an unpleasant once over, as if he'd just walked into the enemy's camp by mistake.

"I'll have to get the mushroom sauce then."

"To drink?" asked Kate as she punched away on an iPad screen.

"A beer." He stopped himself short. Normally, he drank more upscale beer, but at a glance, he didn't think that's what the men, the real men, drank out here. "Whatever you got on tap."

She grabbed a glass and began to fill it.

"Ya want chips?" she asked.

"Sure, and salad."

"Salad bar is over by the door, help ya self."

Kate placed the pint on the bar, leaned over and whispered, "On the house." She pulled away and winked before tallying his bill. "Twenty bucks."

He gulped. That was cheap. For a second, he wondered if it was possibly too cheap, but then he didn't care because he was hungry. He handed over his credit card.

"Blaise... what an unusual name." She swiped his card.

"For some." He'd heard it all before. He typed in his pin.

Kate handed him his card. "You can blaze my trail any time, honey." Her dark eyes were smoldering in the dim light of the front bar.

"Thanks."

Blaise got that comment a lot when out in night-clubs. He knew what those girls were wanting, but they weren't quite as up front like this. "I'll keep that in mind."

"Make sure you do."

Shit, they didn't waste time here. His face reddened, and he picked up his beer and sought solitude over at a table in the back corner.

Blaise took a big gulp of his beer. The cool malt liquid eased his throat and settled his stomach. He'd never experienced anything like this ever before, not even when he traveled overseas. Blaise took another gulp. He had to go easy. Getting drunk was out of the question, but he sure as hell wanted to drink enough to take the edge off the day, so he drank some more before putting the pint down.

Dusty's image came into his mind. Blaise glanced around the pub to see if he could see her. Some of the men were still looking at him, a few men grinned at him. The only women here were the two waitresses.

Part of him was relieved Dusty wasn't here, but part of him was disappointed. Truth be told, he liked a challenge himself. *Put her out of your mind, man.* He drank some more of his beer. It cooled the heat building inside him whenever he thought of Dusty. She was unlike any woman he'd ever met, and for him that was such a turn-on.

He ordered another beer.

"Here, this one's from me." Nat, the other waitress, placed a pint of beer on his table.

"Thanks," said Blaise. He took a big gulp of beer to help blur the events of the day.

"Didn't know ya batted for the other side?"

Blaise looked up and saw Aaron smiling at him with a beer in hand. "I don't."

"What's with the shorts?" Aaron sat down opposite Blaise.

"Gym gear, nothing else to wear." Blaise then realized that was probably the real reason he was getting odd looks from the men in the bar.

Aaron laughed, hard, a little too hard for Blaise's liking. "Mate, ya can't wear that to a country pub."

"No shit." He figured that one out ages ago. *Maybe I*

should check out the local clothing stores in the morning and see what sort of casual clothes I could wear.

"Hey, let me buy you a drink."

"No, that's fine."

"No isn't an option. Make up for me rudely walking out on you."

He nodded to Nat and held up two fingers. Nat grinned as if he'd just asked her out on a date.

"You had to help a neighbor that was a good enough reason to leave."

"Yeah, turned out the bitch didn't really want the sort of help she really needs." Aaron's face clouded over.

"What happened?" Blaise asked tentatively.

He didn't like hearing Dusty being referred to as a bitch.

"Nothing. Fuckin' nothing." He drank the last of his beer. "Hey, you did me a favor by killing one of her sheep."

"I wouldn't say that." Blaise stared coolly at Aaron. He didn't like what he was hearing. Aaron was a client, but this sort of talk lacked any sort of decency. His skin prickled on the back of his neck. *Aaron was bad news.*

"You weren't there. If you were, you'd think the same as me."

"Doubt it." Blaise glared at Aaron. He wasn't about to slag Dusty.

"Hands off him, Aaron. I saw him first," teased Kate as she placed his plate of food on the table.

"Don't worry, Kate, he's all yours. By the way, you don't need to convert him to women, he's already on the right side."

Kate punched Aaron playfully in the shoulder. "You've taken away all the fun."

The steak was huge, double the size at least to what he was used to eating. "There's enough here to feed a small family."

"That's country living for you," said Aaron.

Nat placed the two pints on their table and removed the empties. "Thanks, Nat," said Aaron, his eyes lingering on the front of her low-cut T-shirt. He looked back at Blaise and raised his glass. "To a week in the country."

Blaise did the same. "May it be kinder to me than today."

"Or not." Aaron laughed. "I can show you around if you like."

"The layout of the pub is pretty self-explanatory isn't it?" Blaise began cutting into his steak. He wished he remembered to bring the accounts for Aaron's farm. *The less time spent with this guy, the better.*

"Man, you do have a great sense of humor. I'm talking about the nightlife."

"Not tonight."

Not any night. Not with Aaron revved up like this.

"Come on, you'll enjoy it."

"I'll enjoy going home alone even better."

Things weren't easy with this guy. It didn't help

having drunk two beers quickly on an empty stomach especially after a hot day. Blaise found it hard to concentrate, and he needed his wits. The Aaron sitting opposite him was different to the Aaron he'd seen back at the farm that afternoon.

"Something stronger I reckon for us," said Aaron ignoring Blaise. "Two whiskeys," he yelled to Nat.

Blaise frowned. *Whatever Dusty did to this guy has really rattled him.* Though Blaise wasn't surprised. He was pretty unhinged himself after the encounter with Dusty. Then, so he should've been after driving too fast near sheep. *Maybe something else happened?* Suddenly, Blaise was worried whether or not Dusty was all right. It wasn't his business.

Nat put two glasses of whiskey on the table disrupting Blaise's thoughts.

"Bring the bottle," said Aaron.

Blaise's stomach dropped. Dealing with Aaron like this wasn't going to be easy.

"Bottom's up." Aaron lifted his glass and waited for Blaise to do the same.

"Cheers." Blaise reluctantly clicked his glass with Aaron's and downed the brown liquid in one mouthful. A fire trailed down his insides. His mind fogged, and his body numbed. All at once, he felt much better.

CHAPTER 6

Dusty waved her hands and hooted to encourage the ewes to move into the shed. The ewes were being stubborn and weren't moving. The shearers would be arriving soon, and she wasn't ready. The sky had just begun to lighten as the sun got ready to make an appearance. The day was already getting warm.

Dusty had been slow doing the morning chores, collecting eggs, feeding the dogs and cats. Her jaw hurt, and she was conscious of the purple shade that had bloomed on her cheek. The ache reminded her of Aaron. She clenched her jaw. A bolt of pain shot through her, and she relaxed her mouth.

Ted barked. The ewes yielded and ran up the wooden ramp into the shed. Her whole body ached as she ran up behind them and pulled the gate shut before any of them could change their minds and run back down. Aaron's outburst left her feeling like she'd been run over by a tractor and having to get up at five this morning hadn't helped either.

At least her mom hadn't questioned her too closely last night when she came in, and simply got the plate of food she'd put aside from the fridge and heated it up in the microwave. Dusty did notice there wasn't an extra plate of food for Aaron in the fridge by the time she'd come inside. Her mom would've heard the motorbike roaring away. She was sure her mom knew something happened, but she wasn't ready to fill her in on the details. Dusty just wanted to forget it ever happened.

"Do you need me to help out in the shed?" Dusty's mom had asked her last night. It was the closest they came to discussing Aaron.

She couldn't let her mom work in the shed. It was going to be too hot, and with her new hip, her mom would be pushing herself too much. Her mom had already been cooking all day. Scones, Jubilee cake, and Anzac biscuits were ready to feed the shearers over the next few days.

Dusty couldn't ask her mom to do more. She'd make do, get on with the work, and hopefully, in the meantime, she'd come up with a brilliant idea of who she could ask for help—someone she could trust and someone who didn't have their manhood threatened from having to work for a woman. She paused. Acid rose to her mouth. Or someone who wasn't going to threaten her physically. *Who to ask?* Her mind was all clouded, and she couldn't think.

Dusty moved between the ewes making her way through the square pens toward the other side of the shed. She hoped it wouldn't take long for the dust to cover her pale skin and disguise the evidence. The last thing she wanted to do was have to explain the bruise to the shearers who were always full of questions.

What would she say?

Slipped?

Fell?

No, the truth.

She wasn't about to be a victim.

If anyone asked, she'd tell them Aaron couldn't control his anger. He was known for his temper. She didn't care if they believed her or not. His actions last night confirmed the doubt that had been twisting in her gut. He was no good for her.

She pushed through the swinging door that divided off the last third of the shed into the area for shearing. In this section, there were floorboards instead of grating, an oval metal table that moved around and had a grate-like top for sorting out the fleeces, and an electronic wool baler.

Dusty turned on the industrial fan and stood in front of the moving air, wind in her face like the dogs did when they were on the back of the ute. If only the past twenty-four hours could be blown away. Between Aaron disrupting her sleep and the mystery man who had also made an entrance in her mind, wearing his sexy suit, she felt tired.

A ute rumbled down the driveway. The shearers were here. *Time to get started.* Dusty turned on the electric wool baler, filled up the urn, and set it to a low simmer. Even though it was hot, the shearers would still be looking to have a cuppa in a few hours when they had a break.

She wasn't sure how she was going to do this. There were two shearers and only her acting as shed hand and wool classer. This was going to push her to the edge physically and mentally.

Dusty suppressed a yawn as the shed door slid open. Jim and Mike walked in dressed in matching blue singlets and blue shearing trousers.

"Mornin', boys, ready to get going?"

"Mornin', Dusty, can't wait. Shame about the heat," said Jim. His tall and skinny build made it look like he didn't have the strength to shear a sheep. He was the head shearer even though there were only two of them. Mike was his apprentice.

"Should be cooler tomorrow."

"That'll help, want to be at Port Augusta by next week." He dumped his eighties sports bag in the corner, which was frayed and old and looked like it was about to fall to pieces.

"Fine with me as long as you get my girls shorn. How long do you think you'll shear today?"

"Dunno. It's warming up quick. But if it keeps below thirty-five, we'll shear to five."

"Let's hope the temperature doesn't climb too much then." She walked over and turned on the ceiling fan. It didn't do much, but it was better than nothing. The shed was a metal oven and heated naturally, and there was nothing to do to avoid that. Inside, it was close to fifty degrees.

"Has your mom been cooking?" asked Mike.

"Settle down, boy," said Jim.

He sat down on the old wooden chair and took off his thongs and put on his shearing boots. They were made of soft leather and lined with wool so they looked more like slippers. "He's been salivating all morning over ya mother's cooking."

Dusty smiled. "Yeah, she's been cooking up a storm."

"Great." Mike grinned. "Motivation enough for me."

"Hey, where's ya man?" asked Jim. He stood up stamping his feet to make sure his boots were on correctly.

"He ain't my man," answered Dusty abruptly. She went over to the other side of the area to the bar fridge that sat on top of an old cupboard and took out the vaccination bag.

"It's just you, then?" Mike was about Dusty's age. He stood attaching a comb to the shearing handle.

She knew they weren't going to be happy to hear

that she was the only one in the shed. If she was too slow, then that would put them behind. "Just me."

"You think you can keep up?" asked Mike.

"Just watch me." She hung the vaccination bag near the shearing station. "You boys ready, then?"

"Nearly," said Jim as he adjusted his shearing handle.

Dusty walked over close to them and stood ready to inject the first ewe brought out.

"I'll be impressed if you can keep up," said Mike.

Jim glared at him, but Mike didn't pick up on the vibes.

Dusty braced herself. *Don't take it personally. It's just for a few hours.* Nearly eight hours to be precise, and that was one too many minutes for her already tired body.

"I think I'll shear more sheep than you this morning, Jimbo," said Mike disappearing through the swinging door to grab a sheep.

"Don't ya bet on it, boy." Jim went through a similar door near his station.

Mike dragged out the first sheep, and Dusty kneeled down and injected the vaccine into the fleshy skin near her udder before he'd pulled the cord to turn on his electric shears. She turned quickly and did the same to Jim's sheep, then she hung the bag and needle on the wall, and got ready to collect the belly wool which was kept separate because of its poor quality since it was full of prickles, sweat stains, and feces.

Dusty had about two minutes to wait until Mike finished his sheep first as he pushed the ewe through the small door behind him. Dusty bent down, picked up the fleece, turned and threw it on the table. The fleece flung out and unfolded across the table while loose wool floated down like feathers. Dusty kept focused, grabbed the broom and managed a quick sweep before Mike came back out with another sheep. She didn't have time to inject the ewe because Jim finished his first sheep, and she had to move the fleece out of the way.

How am I going to keep up?

"Bit slow, hey, old boy," yelled Mike to Jim.

"You'll tire out, slow and steady wins the race. Slow and steady." Jim went back out to get another ewe.

Dusty was already behind, and she couldn't put this fleece on the table without classing the other fleece first. She moved it aside, swept away the loose wool before being pushed aside by Jim as he returned. She injected the sheep, then picked up the belly wool and throwing it over into the old-style baler used back in the times of her great grandpa.

This time, instead of waiting for them to finish, she pulled off any dirty wool from the fleece on the table. She pulled off a lock to test its strength and measured its length against her fingers. Deciding it was top quality, she bundled it up and shoved it into the electric baler. Then she ran over and picked up the second fleece to throw on the table just as Mike was finishing his second sheep.

I'm going to have to be quicker.

Dusty was already sweating, her shirt clung to her back, wool stuck to her hair, and her hands were already blackening with lanolin.

The fan moved the air in the shed, but she could hardly feel it as she worked. She kept going, there was nothing else she could do. It didn't matter if a few fleeces piled up on the floor. She'd get to them. As long as the shearers could keep shearing, that meant the job would be done.

"Tired yet?" asked Mike as she leaned down to inject the ewe.

"Not even close." She'd gone beyond tired. Determination kept her going—steel-eyed, she pushed herself to keep working. This was her farm, the wool her income, and she wanted to make it a success. Dusty wasn't about to let a tool like Aaron upset her or put a glitch in the works because he didn't have the balls to keep his desires to himself, or understand that no is no. *Or a stupid city boy or any other man.*

Dusty picked up another fleece and threw it onto the table as a few white pieces of wool fluttered down around her.

CHAPTER 7

Persistent knocking woke Blaise. He rolled over and tried to go back to sleep, but the banging on the door continued.

"Oi. You in there?" A series of thuds hit the door. "City boy, come and get your breakfast." More thudding. Blaise drifted on the edge of sleep. "Don't make me come in there."

The last few words filtered through to his mind and an internal alarm went off. He bolted upright and met the morning as if he'd hit a wall. He groaned. Last night consisted of one too many drinks, and now his head pounded with regret.

He rolled out of bed and remembered he wasn't wearing any clothes. He grabbed the towel from the floor and wrapped it around his waist before opening the door.

"About bloody time," said Beryl with a thunderous

glare that caused him to tremor inside. His breakfast was hidden under a silver cloche on a wooden tray.

"Thank you." He smiled hoping to ease her anger as he took the tray.

"I thought you needed a sleep in since you came home so late last night. Don't let this happen tomorrow morning." Her glare didn't soften. "Towels are the new fashion?" She turned away.

Blaise flushed with embarrassment as he kicked the door closed. The smell of eggs and bacon turned his stomach. He placed the tray on the small table.

The first thing he really needed to do was to rehydrate. He drank a glass of water, sat on the bed, and tried to wake up. The LED on the radio clock flashed eight-thirty. He needed that little bit extra sleep, but he should've already been up. Now, it looked like he wasn't going to have enough time to get into town to buy clothes.

The night with Aaron hadn't been easy. The guy was on a mission of recklessness which Blaise had to work overtime not to be part of. It was bad enough that he'd driven back to the motel. He rubbed his head trying to remember if he'd driven home incident free. *I think so.*

Blaise ate, showered, and dressed into his clean suit. He couldn't go visiting in his gym clothes. *I'll have to get clothes later.* The last thing he wanted to do was create a poor impression with clients by arriving late.

This day is going to be better than yesterday, he told

himself. He couldn't afford to endure another day of mishaps. At least he knew what to do now when he saw a mob of sheep on the road. He packed his briefcase ready to see his first client of the day—the Bakers.

Then he remembered the GPS went flat, and he hadn't looked for the cord last night. "Damn."

Minor issue, he told himself.

Blaise searched through his bag, glad he at least had the foresight to print out the instructions Tim Baker emailed him.

Go out on the main road south of town. After about 5Ks, turn right at the intersection at Tinworth, can't miss it. Follow the road, take the third left, mind the ditch in the road, and keep going until you get to our farm on the right. Oh, and mind your speed on the main road out of town, coppers tend to be there.

Blaise re-read the instructions. He didn't fancy his chances of finding the Baker's farm before dinner tonight.

Nine thirty marked the end of the first session of shearing. The shearers enjoyed her mom's food while Dusty kept working, counting shorn sheep, filling up pens, and classing the few fleeces she'd left on the floor for when she had a moment to catch up. Her body worked automatically. This was the work she'd been doing all her life ever since she could walk.

Her arms and legs ached, and she didn't know how on earth she was going to survive the next two hours before the lunch break. The shearers were slow on account of the heat. Dusty worried they would end up leaving without finishing. Jobs up north were bigger and meant more money, so they weren't going to hang around with a small-time farmer like herself.

Dusty pushed the thoughts away as she stuffed the last fleece into the baler and pressed the lever, causing the metal grill to move downward compressing the wool tightly.

"Come and have a tea," said her mom from the old kitchen table set up in the far corner.

"In a minute." She pressed the lever again to make sure the wool was compacted tight.

"We could do with a few extra minutes' break on account of the heat, so come and take a break," said Jim.

"In a sec."

She was glad the shearers were accommodating, but having a break wasn't quite what she had time for. Besides, if she sat down, she'd be too tired to get up again.

Dusty walked over to the sink washing her hands and

forearms right up to her elbows. The water turned a grimy brown from the lanolin, grease, and dirt. She washed her face, the cool water refreshed her for about ten seconds before tiredness resettled in her facial muscles.

"Tea?" asked her mom.

Dusty nodded her head. Coffee would be better, more caffeine, but there was something refreshing about a cup of black tea after physical work. She found a clean part of the towel and dried her hands.

"Ewes are looking healthy," said Jim as she sat down at the table.

"Thanks." Dusty picked up a slice of Jubilee cake. She looked at the clock, 9:55 a.m. She had five minutes before smoko ended. She had to think of someone to ask to come in and help out on the floor. Otherwise, she was going to crash in a heap.

"They'd be better if they were smaller. Good merinos are heavy," said Mike.

"Toughen up, boy," said Jim.

Dusty's mom handed her a mug of steaming tea. Black, no sugar, and strong. Dusty took a sip.

"I can stay and help for a little bit," said Dusty's mom.

This was the last thing that Dusty wanted her mom to be doing at her age, but it was obvious she needed help. "Okay. But don't you go overdoing it." She gave a stern look at her mother.

"We'll slow down for you, Claire," said Mike.

"That's Mrs. Miller to you, show some respect," said Jim. "I dunno about these young boys."

"Aw, Jimbo, we ain't bad."

"Claire's just fine. You boys won't have to go slow on my account. There's plenty of energy still left in this old dog."

Dusty finished eating the cake, then took a half a sandwich—silverside beef, corn relish with some lettuce—her favorite during shearing time. She had about a minute to refuel and get back to business.

Now that she was sitting down and taking a rest, her mind wandered right back to the man wearing a suit. The more she thought about him, the less angry she was, which wasn't right after what he'd done. She shook her head. She could do without a rest if she was going to think of that city boy. "Right, back into it."

BLAISE STOPPED the car and looked down the long, straight road ahead. He was completely and utterly lost. *How the hell am I going to find my way to visit with clients?* It took him about half an hour to try and find the 'main road' from town. His idea of a main road was a very different one to what was called a main road around here. *If only I'd recharged the damn GPS last night.*

The idea of ringing the client to say he was lost was bad enough, but the real problem was trying to describe where he was so someone could give him directions. Every dirt road out here looked the same, and there were no signs because most of these roads weren't even named. The main distinguishing land-marks were flat brown paddocks, some with sheep, a few eucalyptus trees, and other scrub trees that he had no idea of their name.

There was no other choice. He took out his phone. "You've got to be joking." The screen flashed at him with an exclamation mark surrounded in red—he could only make emergency calls. "This *is* a bloody emergency." He wasn't even sure if he could find his way back into town.

Shit, I don't even know which direction town is in.

He put his car into gear.

I'll drive until I find a farm.

Within five minutes, he came to an intersection. "What's with the lack of signs?" *Left, right, or straight ahead?* He decided to go left. Left had been one of the directions the client had given him, so had right, but he'd turned right at the last intersection. Now he wasn't so sure, maybe he'd turned left? *Just keep driving.* He drove slowly, hunched close to the steering wheel, looking out at the flat, dry landscape for a house.

At the next intersection, there was a sign, but it had bullet holes through it and he couldn't read it. "That'd be right." Not that it would've mattered too much if he could read it, but then if he did manage to get some coverage on his phone, he could tell Tim Baker what road he was on. He decided to go straight ahead.

Blaise drove for another half an hour. Frustration prickled his skin. He was annoyed at himself. This wasn't going to bode well for getting a junior partnership. He didn't want to come out here for a week and get nothing for his trouble.

At the next intersection, he stopped in the middle so he could get a better direction of what was on either side. Trees, paddocks, and more bloody paddocks were all he expected to see, but he stopped to look anyway.

"Bingo." In the distance, he saw a house to the right. He drove toward the farmhouse and turned into a very long driveway lined with native trees.

The house was on the left, and he was about to park there, but then he saw two utes parked next to a shed straight ahead a few hundred meters. From what he experienced at Aaron's, he guessed that was where people would be rather than at the house.

Hey, I'm learning how things work out here.

He parked his German designed car next to the ute and got out. A foreboding flooding through his body—he felt out of place, out of time, and like he didn't belong here at all. An intruder, that's what he felt like. An alien who landed on the wrong planet. He walked up the nearest ramp, pushed open the sliding galvanized door, which gave a metal screech as it opened. A shiver ran over his skin.

"Hello?" he asked as his eyes adjusted to the dull

light from stepping in from full sunlight. The acidic smell hit him, and he had to force himself to keep breathing.

"Come in," said someone from deep within.

Blaise felt a bit better like he was going to get a warm welcome, rather than a chilly one.

Blaise only managed one step forward before someone blocked his way. His eyes were slow to focus in the dim light.

"What the fuck are you doing here?"

The words stung him. Blaise stood looking at *her* for a few seconds before he processed who had spoken.

It was the women who kept haunting his mind. *Dusty.*

The last person he expected to see today, even though he secretly hoped to. Dusty stood looking at him, a fire in her eyes caused him to freeze, but one that also stirred a deeper fire within him.

"I said, what the fuck are you doing here?"

CHAPTER 8

Dusty couldn't believe who had just walked into her shearing shed. Her anger spiked, then plummeted and swirled in a mixture of contradicting emotions. He was the last person she ever wanted to see again. Even though he looked sexier wearing today's suit. He was completely out of place, standing there awkwardly, but that made him more appealing, made him different to the men she was used to.

Best to send him packing, she thought.

"I'm lost." Blaise stammered. His face flushed a deep red as he looked at her.

"Really?" Dusty stood glaring at him, her hands rested on her hips. She found it hard to stay angry at him. *After what he did...* even the lost expression on his face was endearing.

"Yes." He wiped his forehead nervously.

"Is that someone come to give us a hand?" yelled Mike.

Dusty resisted the urge to yell back to tell Mike to mind his business. This was her shed, and she was going to run it the way she wanted to. Attraction aside, the bottom line was that this man wasn't fit to stay in her shed because he had no idea of how to act around animals.

"New suit?"

"Yes. I like to look my best." His hand ran down the length of this blue patterned tie making sure it was straight and neat.

"We can do with some help," yelled Jim. "Can he work in the shed?"

Dusty's temper increased, and she took a deep breath to stop herself from boiling over.

Claire stepped up. "Now are you going to introduce me to this smart-looking man?"

Dusty narrowed her eyes at her mom. Claire ignored her and stretched out her hand. "I'm Claire."

"Blaise Johns, pleased to meet you." Blaise shook her hand.

"Likewise."

"He was just leaving," said Dusty.

"Well, no... not exactly," said Blaise. "I need some directions first."

"Turn around, walk out the door, get in your car, and drive away," said Dusty. "Simple."

"Ignore her, she's just overworked," said Claire. "Where are you wanting to go?"

"Bakers. You know them?"

"Please, Mom, we've got to get started," said Dusty. She couldn't believe this man was still here. *Blaise.* His name rolled around in her mind as if not wanting to be forgotten.

"This won't take long," said Claire. She turned to Blaise. "Course we know them."

Blaise smiled. "Finally, something is working in my favor."

"Mine, too, you'll be gone soon then we can get back to work. You do seem to be good at disrupting my life."

Blaise looked at Dusty. His blue eyes meet hers, and she held her breath. The intensity in his eyes stared right through the front she was putting on, right into her heart which responded by pounding faster.

"I can stay and help," offered Blaise.

"That will be—" began Claire.

"No," interrupted Dusty.

"Look, I'm really sorry what happened yesterday. Let me make it up to you by working in your shed today."

"What happened yesterday?" asked Claire looked suspiciously at her daughter.

"Nothing." Dusty glared at Blaise. "I told you not to worry about it."

"Well, I'm worrying about it. I owe you the price of

a sheep, which you won't accept, so let me work for you for a day then we can call it quits."

"I don't think... "

"Dusty, let him work, he looks strong, and we need the help," said Claire.

Her mom was going to stay and help out, but she really needed to go back to the house and begin preparing the shearers' lunch.

Dusty sighed, her anger rippled out with her breath. Her mom was right. She needed the help. The shearers doubted she could keep this level of work up, and soon enough, she was going to collapse in a heap. She needed help. She'd been secretly asking for help for the last two hours trying to work out who to ask. The Hancock boys were away, the Thorne boy was too young, and there were a few boys from town, but they would have to be trained, and that was the last thing she felt like doing. Dusty knew she was being too picky.

"Fine then. One day, and only one day, and if you annoy me and I tell you to walk, then you walk. Got it?"

"Got it."

BLAISE ROLLED UP HIS SLEEVES. The gym gear would've been the ideal attire for this morning after all. He couldn't believe what he was volunteering for. *Can I survive a day of shearing?* But he had to do this. He had to make amends, and this was the only way he could see himself doing this.

Dusty didn't deserve to be out of pocket because of him. She looked exhausted. A shade of purple on her cheek hidden under a smear of dirt caught his attention. *Someone hit her?* He knew Aaron helped her yesterday, and he was revved up at the pub last night. *Could it have been Aaron?* It made sense. Despite the prickly welcome he received from her, he found himself wanting to protect her, take some of the load. He also wanted to punch Aaron next time he saw him.

"Let's see if my gym workouts have paid off." He smiled, feeling his confidence increase. *At least I'm fit.*

"Yes, let's see." Dusty's stare caused doubt to drown the moment of confidence he'd found. "Don't get cocky. You've got no idea what you're up for."

"Okay," he squeaked.

This woman managed to squeeze his balls with words and a simple glare. Instead of running away, he wanted to find out more about her. Something in her light blue eyes suggested that this wasn't the real her, which only spurred his curiosity to find out more about her.

"I just got to makes some calls to let people know I won't be coming today." He wasn't sure that would work since he didn't have any coverage, but maybe he'd get a bar or two of reception out here.

"I can call them," said Claire.

"I don't know." Client confidentiality was important. "You don't know who to call."

"Well, you were on your way to Tim Baker's place, you're then going up to see Hancock's, and after lunch you were going out to Bluey's Mechanics on the other side of town."

Shit. He stared at her with his mouth open. *How did she know all of that?*

"Don't worry, they won't mind me calling." Claire patted him on the shoulder as she walked out of the shed. She balanced three Tupperware containers on her hip. "Shut your mouth, don't want a fly finding its way to your tonsils."

"Okay, then."

He wasn't about to tell Danny about this. He didn't think he'd be happy about Claire calling his clients and telling him that he wasn't coming to see them today which had been the whole purpose of this trip. *It's only one day. I'll make up the time lost, and I can still have a chance at junior partner.*

Blaise looked around the shed. The shearers were grinning ear to ear as they disappeared through separate swinging doors. *Where are they going?* He wondered what he should do first. He walked over to the center of the area guessing this would be a good start.

"Here." Dusty handed him a broom. He took it. She didn't look happy. He contemplated what he should do with the broom, other than to sweep. There seemed to be a layer of permanent dust on the floor, and there were bits of wool everywhere, and surely a vacuum would be a better option.

"You do know how to use a broom, don't you?" she asked.

"Of course." But not where specifically he was meant to use the broom in the shed. He thought there was something obvious he'd missed. Her face looked like a dust storm hit, and he wanted to keep his balls intact so he didn't ask.

Dusty sighed. "I don't know about this."

"It's the least I can do."

One day in the shed he hoped would square things between them. *Hopefully, I can get to know Dusty a little better?*

He looked at her. Tight jeans clung to her hips giving him some eye candy. She wore a checked short-sleeved shirt, the top button was undone, and he could see her tanned neck glistening with sweat. His heart quickened. When she moved, he glimpsed paler skin through the opening of the shirt. Her hair was tied back, and it was full of pieces of wool and dirt. She looked gorgeous. He swallowed hard. *Keep it together,* he warned himself. *One step at a time.*

"When the shearers have finished, you sweep away the loose wool under the table here," Dusty instructed.

Easy. He smiled. She gave him a thunderous stare. He lost his smile and kept his eyes meeting her stormy ones, enjoying the glint of danger there, which stirred a different sort of storm within him.

The shearers dragged out a sheep on its backside and pulled the chords, bringing the shears to life. The two electric shears buzzed like a storm of bees. He realized that she'd been speaking. He could barely hear her over the noise.

"What?" He gripped the stick of the broom to help settle his nerves.

One of the shearers threw a piece of wool in their direction. Without looking, Dusty caught it and held it up to him. "Belly wool. You put it over here." She took a few steps and threw the wool in a metal container or whatever it was. "I'll inject for now until you get a handle on things, then maybe you'll get promoted."

Great. The last thing he wanted to be doing was injecting a sheep. He stood waiting.

The other shearer threw something at him. Damp wool wrapped around his face, dirt flew into his eyes and mouth. For a second, he thought he was going to suffocate, and then the wool fell away. Dusty stood glaring at him.

Blaise knew he'd failed the first step. *Great. Just bloody great.* He took the piece of wool from her and threw it over to the container thingy. It went about a meter, hung in the air for a bit and then fell short. Way short. He made a mental note that wool wasn't like a football.

He walked over quickly, dragging the broom with

him, and picked up the wool and dumped it into the container thingy. He turned around, and the first sheep was being ushered out through a gap behind the shearer, naked, its wool on the ground.

Dusty squatted, grabbed the fleece, and swiftly threw it. He checked out her tight bum. His view was over all too quickly when she stood up and threw the fleece. He jumped thinking it was about to land on him, but it floated down onto the table like a blanket on a bed.

"Sweep," she yelled.

Shit. Blaise rushed forward and swept away the loose wool but only managed two sweeps before the shearer dragged out another sheep, and he was pushed out of the way.

Shit. They were quick.

Dusty stopped whatever it was she was doing at the table with the fleece, picked up the needle and injected, just as the other shearer finished another sheep. She picked up the fleece before he remembered he had about two seconds to sweep the floor, and he'd better hurry.

Two jobs. That was all he had to do, and he wasn't keeping up.

In the meantime, Dusty had done about twenty jobs. He couldn't believe how hard everyone worked, and they made it look easy.

Sweat dribbled down his back. Blaise felt as if he had wading pools under each of his arms. His second and clean suit was going to need about three rounds of dry cleaning before it could be worn again.

Another sheep was finished. Blaise swept away the wool, collected the belly wool, swept, belly wool, swept. He was getting the hang of this and began to feel chuffed. He could do a day's work in the shed, no worries. He'd even give the injecting a go if Dusty asked.

She paused next to him. His mind went into over-drive as he smelled her faint floral scent mixed with her sweat. A strand of hair stuck to her cheek begging for him to reach over and brush it out of the way.

"Just one more thing," she said.

Lines on her face relaxed since he'd arrived. Blaise hoped it was because of him.

He held his breath. His heart pounded a different rhythm being so close to her. He was becoming intoxicated on her scent.

"Lose the tie."

CHAPTER 9

"So, will ya be back tomorra?" Mike brushed down his shears. An unlit cigarette balanced on his lips.

"Not sure if the lady of the house will have me," answered Blaise.

He stood in the old wool baler pushing wool down with his legs, apparently this was the old-fashion way. He'd stopped worrying about his expensive suit hours ago figuring it would dry clean up all right, or if not, then he'd just have to buy another one. He didn't care as long as he got to be around Dusty.

Blaise could barely feel his body anymore. He ached all over, every muscle. He did doubt whether or not to keep paying his gym membership. In six hours of work, he'd tightened and strengthened his muscles to the equivalent of over a year of working out three times a week. Sweat dribbled down the side of his face, but he kept working. Dusty hadn't stopped all day, so if she could keep going, there was no way he was going to let up. That would be embarrassing.

"I'm sure she'll have you," interjected Jim as he oiled the shearing handle.

"Oi, I can hear you," yelled Dusty from the other side of the divide counting sheep.

The shearers laughed. Blaise smiled and looked down at his feet disappearing into the wool.

"We want ya to hear 'cause we want ya to know that you should keep hold of this guy. He sure as hell is a good worker," yelled Jim.

Dusty didn't answer. Instead, a thud echoed from where she worked as she slammed a gate shut. Blaise grinned. *There's a chance with her.* He could feel it in his bones.

He jumped down from the old baler and cringed as his entire body complained from the sudden movement. He was already tightening up. *I'm not going to be able to walk tomorrow.*

Guilt still churned in his gut. *Another day?* There was the real world he had to consider. He needed to visit clients, twice as many now to make up for today. He had a real job to keep, and it wasn't helping him get a promotion by playing at being a shed hand.

"Well, I think we can do without him," said Dusty.

She walked through the swinging door and then over to the kitchen table. She flicked open a dirty book and wrote down the figures.

Her words caused a sinking sensation to wash over

him. A small spark inside his heart fluttered. *It's not over yet.*

"I can help out if you like," said Blaise.

What am I saying? Suddenly, the idea of not being here tomorrow and not seeing Dusty again made him nervous. He wanted to at least get to know her. She'd softened toward him during the day, and he wanted to pursue this potential further.

"Fifteen and eleven." Dusty ignored Blaise.

"Fifteen my way?" asked Mike.

"Yes."

Jim groaned. Mike let out a whoop of joy. "About time I got ahead of you, old man," said Mike.

"I said I can help you," Blaise stated. "The day isn't over." He was sure there were jobs that needed to be done today, and if he couldn't manage it tomorrow, then the least he could do was to help out now. Plus, if he could help out Dusty with no one else around, maybe he could get her to loosen up, and there could be a chance to get to know her.

Dusty closed the book and walked over to the urn and switched it off. She packed away the tea and sugar in airtight containers and shelved them in the glass-door cupboards fixed to the wall.

Blaise stood staring at her waiting for an answer. *Why do I bother?* But there was something about her which made him stay. Something he'd never experienced before. His curiosity sparked as he waited, hoping she'd answer him.

He allowed his eyes to casually wander over her body. Her arm muscles were toned and tanned. He could imagine his fingers sliding along her skin causing it to goosebump.

"Come on, boy, grab ya things. We'll let them sort this out." Jim stood up, stretched his stiff body, and grabbed his ancient sports bag. When Mike didn't move, he pulled the younger boy up by the collar of his T-shirt. "Come on."

"See ya tommora, Blaise." Mike couldn't help himself. He grinned like he was the best comedian this side of Adelaide.

"Not unless I do away with you first for these stupid comments." Jim pushed Mike forward toward the door. "See ya."

"Bye." Blaise turned back to Dusty. "Is there anything else you want me to do?" He wasn't going to give in. She needed help and despite being sore and tired, he'd step up and offer his assistance. He knew she wasn't hopeless or not capable, but something inside of him wanted to protect her, and this was the only way he knew how to do it right now.

Dusty took a deep breath and turned around. He saw the tiredness in her eyes, like a thick, soupy foggy winter's morning. He softened his voice. "Let me finish the day's work at least."

He had to remind himself maybe she wasn't interested in him, and hell, that was hardly surprising. Her shoulders slumped. Still, Blaise hung on the little hope that was there because so far, she hadn't said straight out no.

DUSTY WASN'T sure how Blaise managed to make it through the day without igniting her temper. What was on the tip of her tongue was to tell him to stay. She hated to admit it, but he'd done all right. The words of praise stuck in her throat.

She looked at Blaise, soaking in his image. His sexy suit looked worse for wear now with brown stains and bits of wool clinging to the material. Her pulse increased. His black hair was damp with sweat. She resisted the urge to go and pull the pieces of wool from his hair.

His head dropped. "Okay, I'll go then."

"No." Dusty stepped forward to grab his arm to stop him. Then pulled back embarrassed by her action. She didn't want to give him any hope that there was something between them, ever, even though her body reacted as if it would. They were from different worlds, and sooner or later he'd go back to the city, and she would be left alone.

His deep blue eyes looked questioningly at her.

Dusty had to be honest with herself. He'd been just as much help today as Aaron would've been. Better actually, from the point of view he did exactly what she told him to do and never argued. And he hadn't complained once. *Not bad for a boy from the concrete jungle.*

He had stamina, strength, and sex appeal. *God, did he have sex appeal.* That suit should've come off by now, but Dusty managed to get herself in check. She looked away as heat flushed on her checks.

She reminded herself to think about work. Work was the only thing she had time for right now and in the immediate future. She couldn't cope with anything else. Her farm took priority, and she needed help with that. Before she could clock off today, the shorn sheep needed to be returned to the paddocks, and the next mob of sheep moved into the shed. It was like playing a chess game, moving mobs around, in and out of the shed, keeping them separate according to the sire they had been mated to in order to keep track of the bloodlines. "Okay," she said quickly before she changed her mind.

"Okay... what?" asked Blaise. He looked at her with surprise.

"Okay, I need help finishing up today. Mom will give you dinner, then you can be on your way, and we'll consider things settled between us."

"Good, because I want things to be squared, and I love a challenge." He winked at her.

Dusty's mouth went dry, and her heart sped away, thumping out a Morse code, telling her to act with this hot guy standing in front of her. *I can't,* she thought with her head and not her heart.

"Don't get ahead of yourself. We've got to move a few mobs of sheep and finish this before dark."

"Late dinner then." He smiled.

"Only if things go wrong."

Her entire body was numb, and she didn't know how she had the energy to keep standing. She suppressed a yawn. Just a few more jobs before she could have a breather. Then begin again tomorrow.

"Right, ma'am. Where would you like me, and what would you like me to do first?"

A different sort of heat began to rise within Dusty, one that made her think of a few things he could do to her which had nothing to do with farming. "You any good at massages?" *Shit*.

"Yeah?" Blaise looked confused.

She hadn't meant to say that out loud. There were plenty of knots in her neck which could do with firm hands to loosen them up. She imagined Blaise's soft city hands running over her skin. *Get it together.* But her walls were beginning to crumble. This guy was honest and humble, standing in front of her in an expensive wrecked suit still offering to help her. It was endearing. Something she'd never felt with a man before, not at this intensity. There was a different sort of tension between them.

No, she reminded herself. *He's from a different world than me. There's no way it would work.*

"You want me to massage sheep?" asked Blaise.

Dusty let out a sigh. "No, we'd better leave that for another time."

"Some joke for the out-of-towner, is it?"

Dusty laughed. She wasn't sure if he just didn't get it, or if he was being polite and deliberately misunderstood her. "Something like that." She walked over to the door.

Blaise followed. "Well, I'm glad I don't have to massage any sheep, not with you around, you'd be the better option."

Is he flirting with me? Dusty couldn't believe he just said that. *Maybe he's tired like me, and he's not thinking about what he's saying?* She stepped out on the narrow landing of the shed. *Best to get back to finishing the jobs.* That was the safe thing to do.

But his humor had gotten under her skin.

She liked it. She wanted more. *So much more.*

"I want you to stand to the left over there between this shed and the silos." She pointed.

Blaise stepped in front of her, brushing against her body. *Holy hell*, she thought as his body heat blasted her, sending her mind in a whirl of bliss and causing her to think about ripping off his shirt.

He peered around the corner of the shed. "Silos?"

"The round things," said Dusty. She inhaled slowly. He smelled like mixed spice, lanolin, and sweat. *God, he smells great.*

"You just want me to stand there?" He looked back at her over his shoulder.

"Yeah, and wave your hands around to make sure the sheep don't run toward you. I want them to go straight past you and into the paddock there." *Jobs first*, she told herself firmly.

"Easy."

"Yes, so you go get into position and keep an eye out for the sheep."

He turned around and faced her front on. She held her breath. "What position was that you want me in?"

She inhaled sharply. Words caught in her throat as she looked up into his eyes. *Cheeky bastard.*

He grinned. His lips were so kissable. And for a moment, all she thought about doing was reaching up and giving him one hell of a kiss. But her mind kicked into gear. "You know."

He stepped forward. "Remind me."

"Over there by the silos," she managed to whisper, unable to move. She was caught in his gaze. Her skin prickled as he came closer while her mind slipped out of gear.

He stopped just before they touched. She held her ground next to him. The thought of doing any more jobs faded from her mind. Heat rose inside of her. She wanted to place her hands on his chest, slip them under his shirt, and then run her tongue over his salty skin. She swallowed hard.

He began to lift his hands reaching for her.

Her mind snapped back in charge, and she stepped

back. *This isn't right. I don't do this sort of thing with a stranger.*

"Right then, get down there and be ready." She winced at her choice of words. Maybe her mind was more in charge than she wanted it to be.

"Oh, I'll be waiting for you, and I'll be more than ready."

"Good. I like a man who's ready." Dusty stepped back into the shed. *He's a hell of a flirt.* "Don't disappoint me."

"I won't."

She glanced back at him. Her skin prickled pleasantly, he was looking at her. She turned quickly and disappeared into the safety of the shed, hiding her smile from him. She liked the sound of a man who didn't disappoint. Heat flushed through her body. *He won't be around for long*, she reminded herself. Dusty untied the chain around the gate. Her grin was wide, and her heart was light. *He won't be around long, but I might have some fun in the meantime.*

BLAISE STOOD by the silos scuffing his shoe into the ground. *Was she flirting with me?* That whole massage comment hadn't seemed like the ribbing he'd been getting all day. It gave him hope that Dusty wanted to get to know him better. He smiled. That would make this whole week to the country worth the cost of two expensive woolen suits, and possible new leather shoes, and any scratches he might have gotten on the paintwork of his car. He squared his shoulders. *Can't wait to tell the mates what I've been doing.* They weren't going to believe him. He wasn't sure how he'd describe Dusty to them. Mostly, he didn't want to. He wanted to keep her all for himself.

Blaise heard a noise to his right and looked toward the shed. White ewes came into sight. He stood expecting them to run past. He glimpsed Dusty. She looked tired, dirt smeared on her face, but there was also a lightness about her that wasn't there before.

Dusty walked behind the ewes, relaxed and confident, while casually swatting at the flies. He couldn't take his eyes off of her. He was sure something was about to happen between them before when they were on the landing, but then she stepped away. That something rekindled inside of him as he looked at her again.

"Look at the sheep," Dusty yelled at him.

Shit. He turned his attention to the job.

A ewe at the front was walking toward him, the others following behind.

Blaise froze. *What do I do?*

It was too late.

They ran past him ignoring him as if he was only a tree. "Shit." He didn't need to be told that Dusty was about to turn his guts into garters. "Shit."

Blaise stood frozen as the ewes bolted past him. A

few of them jumped into the air and kicked their back legs as if mocking him for not being able to stop them.

"Come back here," he yelled after them.

The ewes kept running straight ahead and out the open gate behind him. *That's got to be bad.* Suddenly, he wished he'd gone when the shearers had left. *What was I thinking?* He knew he hadn't been thinking with his head. He'd been so distracted with Dusty, all he cared about was getting to know her, that and some.

Dusty ran up behind him.

He braced himself.

"You're meant to be helping me," said Dusty.

He could feel the heat of anger radiating from her as she stopped next to him. But she didn't explode like she had early today.

"It's not bloody rocket science, honestly."

"Sorry. I'll run after them and bring them back." He wondered how hard that would actually be. But he had to fix things.

"I should've sent you home." Dusty turned back and ran toward the ute that had been parked behind the shed. His silver Audi looked completely out of place next to her ute.

Blaise ran after her.

"Stay here, out of the bloody way," yelled Dusty as she got into the ute and revved it to life as if she was in a chase movie and the mob was hard on her tail.

Blaise flattened himself against his car so she wouldn't hit him as she reversed the ute quickly. "Shit."

She stopped to put the ute into first gear and leaned out of the window. "Stay here and make sure the sheep don't go toward you when I bring them back. They have to go into the gate near the silos, remember?" The wheels skidded on the loose stone as she took off, one dog barked from the back of the ute, and another raced with the ute heading after the sheep.

Blaise stood coughing in a cloud of dust. "Crazy woman." But she was a crazy woman that had still gotten to him, and there was no way he could put her out of his mind now.

Waiting for the sheep to return, he tried to come up with a better plan. Obviously, standing there to scare the sheep didn't work the first time, and while he was a little relieved that Dusty was going to trust him again, he wasn't so sure he was up for the task. The bit of confidence he'd gained from working in the shed just melted away in the late afternoon sun.

"Think, think."

The sheep would be coming back from the direction of the gate they'd just bolted through. All he had to do was to stop them from running past him. He looked behind him. There was another gate, one that led through a series of pens around the shearing shed. He ran over and shut the gate, at least then if the sheep did get past him, they weren't going to create a bigger problem by going into the pens.

He heard Dusty revving the ute and the dogs barking like mad things out in the paddock. Blaise got into his car and parked where he was meant to stand. *Something bigger would be more likely to stop the sheep from running in this direction.* He got out, left the engine running and stood waiting.

This time he was ready.

Blaise saw the sheep running toward the gate. *I can do this.* He was better with numbers, working through budgets and negative gearing, and not working with animals.

The sheep slowed down at the gate. They stood looking at him.

"Bring it on girls," he said. "Come and take me on."

The sheep weren't moving forward and stood staring at Blaise.

Yeah, I'm scary now. Blaise stood proudly with his effort.

The ute door slammed. "Get back, you're too close," yelled Dusty.

He frowned. "Get back where?"

"Go back a bit," she yelled. Dusty pointed behind him.

Blaise got into his car and reversed back a few meters. Like magic the ewes began to move again. *Unbelievable.* He got out of the car slowly.

Dusty and the dogs followed up behind. Some of the sheep stopped to nibble spilled grain and some fed on weeds by the silos. The mob kept moving closer to the gate until finally they ran into the paddock.

Blaise let out his breath.

Dusty waved for him to follow her. He turned off his car and ran after her.

"That was much better." She smiled. "I'll make a country boy out of you yet." She started walking after the ewes, and Blaise followed relieved he had managed to do something right.

"You can't get too close to them, and if you're too far away, it's not going to do anything," said Dusty.

"Okay. The dogs seem to know where the sheep are going."

"Yeah, they've done this before, hundreds of times. They know the paddocks."

The sheep gained momentum as they ran through another gate. Dusty whistled the dogs back. They came running, tongues hanging out and panting.

"Help me shut the gate, then we'll bring up another mob." The long wire gate perplexed Blaise, but he simply did what he was told and held the star-dropper in the middle to help take up some of the strain.

How she worked amazed him. Dusty made everything look easy, and yet he'd struggled to stop the sheep from going in the wrong direction. Watching her work made it clear to him. There was no doubt he wanted her even more. She radiated confidence and strength, drawing him to her.

Dusty finished securing the gate. "Come on, it's going to be dark soon."

They began walking back toward the shearing shed.

He glanced at her. A new layer of dirt emphasized the tiredness in her face. It made her look even more appealing. He resisted taking her up in his arms and kissing her.

"We've got to move one more mob, then we can do the odd jobs, then have dinner," said Dusty as they walked to the ute.

"I don't have to stay for dinner." Blaise couldn't believe he'd just said that. Of course, he wanted to stay for dinner.

"I'd imagine Mom would've cooked enough food for you, and you've done more than enough work today to earn a meal. Besides, it's getting late. By the time you get back to town, you'll be lucky to get a meal because the kitchens in the pubs will be closed."

"As long as I'm not imposing," said Blaise.

"No, it's nice to have company for a change."

They drove down the paddock where the sheep ran the wrong way, through another gate. The dogs did most of the hard work while Blaise sat in the passenger seat. The heat radiated out from Dusty. The way she worked had sent his mind into a spin which made it hard for him to find the words to ask her out.

"Nearly there," said Dusty.

The sheep knew where to go, unlike the other mob, and they ran to the back of the shed to the pen area. Then they merely circled around as a mob, confused where they were meant to go.

"Why is that gate shut?" asked Dusty.

Blaise's stomach lurked. *Shit I can't do anything right out here.* "Um…"

"You've got to be kidding me?"

Blaise felt a renewed radiation of anger from Dusty. "I'll go and open it."

Before Blaise could get out, the sheep had spied a gap and ran, heading back out to the paddock they came from.

"Bloody hell," said Blaise.

Dusty took a deep breath. "I think it's time you left."

CHAPTER 10

BLAISE DIDN'T NEED to be told twice. But he hesitated with his hand on the ute door. He didn't want to leave her. Then she gave him a thunderous stare. He got out the ute as Dusty sped off. He turned away and went to his car. He'd undone all the hard work with the simplest of tasks. At least, he'd had a chance with her, but now that was completely blown, and he only had himself to blame.

He went to his car, got in and drove slowly down the driveway. *So much for asking her out.* His heart sunk. Despite their differences, and the fact he wasn't sure long-distance relationships were for him, Blaise wanted to see Dusty again.

Something caught his eye by the side of his car, and he skidded to a stop. "Bloody hell."

Claire stood in his way. "Where do you think you're going?"

He pressed the electric window down. "I've not been that helpful."

"Come inside and have some food. Don't worry what Dusty might say. This is my treat, and I won't take no for an answer."

Claire gave a look that was very similar to the one he'd just gotten from Dusty. He swallowed hard. *This is my chance to try again.*

"Okay."

"Good, come on, park your car by the back gate." Claire marched back toward the house.

Blaise did what he was told, parked his car, got out, and it beeped locked.

"Dogs won't steal your car, no need to lock it."

Of course, there wasn't. "Habit."

He wasn't about to change because in three days he was going to be back in the city. If Danny ever wanted him to come back and visit clients again, then there was no way in hell he was going to come. Partnership or not, he knew that country life wasn't for him. He walked through the gate and up the path leading to the back door of the house. If only he could get Dusty out of his mind.

Blaise followed Claire inside. "Take your boots off at the back door, please."

"Sorry."

He'd been so busy trying to erase Dusty from his mind, he'd forgotten about his dirty shoes. Blaise stepped back outside and lifted each foot to look at the bottom. The soles of his shoes were encrusted with sheep shit and wool plus the odd small stone. He sighed. *Maybe staying to help out wasn't such a good idea.* With effort because his legs muscles were strained and tired, he kicked off his shoes and stepped inside wearing his socks.

A stale, acidic smell wafted upward from his feet, and Blaise wrinkled his nose. He wasn't used to so many putrid smells, especially one that was coming from him. He decided the socks should go in the bin when he got back to his motel room.

Blaise wandered into the kitchen. He hadn't eaten so much in one day and still managed to feel hungry at the end of it. The chops smelled great as they hissed and spat in the pan. It took all his self-control not to go over and take one and begin eating it like a caveman.

Before he could sit down, Claire came into the room holding a bundle of clothes. "I think Sam's clothes will fit you, even if they might be a bit big around the waist and too short in the legs, at least, they're clean." She handed him the clothes. "Here's a towel and fresh soap." She handed over the bundle.

"Who's Sam?" Blaise hadn't recalled Dusty mentioning she had a brother. He held the bundle of clothes.

"My late husband. Don't worry, he won't mind you wearing his clothes. I don't need to be hanging onto these forever."

"Oh... I'm sorry."

"Yes, well, it happened about three years ago, and I miss the old bugger to bits. Life goes on, doesn't it? Now, get and have a shower, your dinner will be ready soon." She pointed toward the bathroom. "On your left. Keep it quick. You're washing in rainwater, and it's the middle of summer."

"Thanks." Blaise walked to the bathroom, unsure about wearing Claire's late husband's clothes, and not sure about what Dusty would think of this. He was pretty certain she wouldn't like it one bit. He didn't care. The clothes smelled laundry fresh with a hint of mothballs which was a hell of a lot better than what he smelled like right now.

Blaise closed the door in the quaint-sized bathroom, placed the clean clothes on a footstool, and began peeling off his own clothes. Blaise doubted the smell could ever be washed out, it was so heavy and strong.

He set the shower going and scrubbed his body clean. The hot water soaked the tension from out of his muscles. Mindful of not wanting to use up too much water, he hurried. He was washing his hair with soap when there was a knock on the door.

"Just me, I need to grab the bottle of disinfectant."

Blaise froze. It was Dusty's voice. Before he could yell out 'don't come in,' the door opened.

Shit.

"Wow! You're having a hot shower tonight, leave some hot water for me."

Blaise heard a cabinet door click open. He knew he should say something, but it was like the water washed his voice down the plughole. He stood as far away from the screen as possible with his back to the curtain. *Hopefully, it's not that see-through.*

"It that you, Dusty?" yelled Claire from somewhere in the house.

Blaise heard something fall on the tiles of the bathroom.

"Oh. My. God."

"Dusty?" he asked.

"Yes, it's me." She lowered her voice. "I thought I sent you home."

"Um... well... your mom—"

"Mom will have a bit to answer for." He heard her opening the cabinet door. He wanted to tell her to leave so he could finish his shower in peace.

"Don't you use locks?" she asked.

"Forgot." It was a weak answer, but the truth. All he'd wanted to do was get clean.

"Don't use all the water," said Dusty.

Blaise heard the door close. He let out a sigh followed by a yell. "Shit." Blaise jumped out of the scolding hot water. "Bloody hell." Dusty had left the cold water running in the sink. *Some payback.* He turned off the tap and carefully went back to wash the soap from his hair and any lingering thoughts of Dusty, blasting himself good and proper with cold water.

Blaise walked from the bathroom wearing fresh

clothes and smelling of soap. Dusty was nowhere to be seen. She was still in his mind. He liked her cheeky flair, it kept him on his toes. Matched with his wit, they could have a good time together. If only they could get over coming from different worlds. *Damn her.* He couldn't stop thinking about her.

He hitched the trousers up, they were meant for a large waist. *Damn me.* Something about Dusty made him nervous, a good sort of nervous, and she didn't fit into his usual idea of what women did. That was tantalizingly refreshing but also downright frustrating.

"Come and take a seat," said Claire as Blaise walked into the kitchen.

He didn't need to be told twice. He suppressed a yawn as Claire placed a plate full of food, chops with thick homemade mushroom sauce, mashed potatoes, carrots, and a few peas which he didn't like, but he wasn't about to complain. Right now, he'd eat anything.

"Thanks, this is great." Blaise tried not to talk with his mouth full.

"Sorry, it's nothing flashy. If we weren't shearing, I'd cook up a roast." Claire stood at the sink wiping dishes.

"This is perfect." Blaise had to force himself to eat slower. He was shoving food in his mouth like he'd been stranded on an island without food for months rather than hours. "I can't believe how much I've eaten today."

"That's farm work for you."

"I don't think I'm cut out for it."

"You didn't do too badly from what Dusty told me."

"Really?" Blaise nearly dropped his knife and fork in shock. "She really said that."

"Well, she did say you didn't do too bad for a city toff."

That sounded more accurate. "I made a mess of things this afternoon."

"Don't worry, Dusty got the sheep in all right. Shearing will go on tomorrow, and she'll forget your wrongs soon enough."

Blaise doubted it. He scraped the last of the peas onto his fork. Not wanting to offend Claire's warm hospitality, he made sure his plate was super clean. "Thanks again." He placed his knife and fork parallel on his plate to indicate he'd finished. It was the sort of behavior he did when eating at a five-star restaurant.

"Dessert?"

"I should get going really." He suppressed another yawn. He hadn't felt this tired since, since he couldn't even remember ever feeling so exhausted in all his life. "I don't think I could eat any more." His stomach was pleasantly full, and his eyes were becoming heavy.

"Tea or coffee?"

"Coffee." He needed a caffeine hit to wake up enough to drive back to the motel. He was dreading the trip in the dark, and he doubted that he'd be able to find his way home at all.

Claire went over and put the kettle on to boil. "How

about you go out to the lounge, and I'll bring you a coffee."

"Sure."

"Down the hallway, second door on the left."

"Thanks." Half asleep, Blaise walked down the hallway, opened the door, found the light switch. He'd barely sat on the lounge when he was already asleep, snoring ever so slightly.

"WHAT DO you think you were doing asking him to stay?" Dusty demanded as she came back inside from finishing the evening chores. The back door slammed heavy behind her.

"Shush," said Claire.

She took Dusty's meal out from the oven and placed it on the kitchen table.

"Don't shush me. What are you playing at Mom?"

Dusty put her hands on her hips. She couldn't help think her mom was trying to set her up with Blaise. *Don't know why. He'll be going back to the city in a few days.*

"You needn't be so harsh, Dusty. Blaise worked hard today, give him a break." She closed the oven door. "He's doing all right considering he knows nothing about farming."

"I'm the one who needs a break." It was dark

outside, and she literally had to drag herself back to the house before falling asleep in the ute.

"Yes, you do, and you should consider taking time off after shearing."

Dusty sighed. After shearing, there'd be a few weeks of downtime, but she'd already planned catching up on odd jobs around the farm. Some of the fences needed mending, then she had to look over the tractor and seeding equipment to get it ready for when the rains came. A holiday was the furthest thing from her mind. "Well, maybe next year."

"Next year, my foot." She raised an eyebrow at Dusty.

"Still, you haven't answered my question." Dusty started eating. "Why is Blaise still here?"

"I couldn't send him away when he could barely stay awake. You want to have to deal with the guilt of him having an accident on the way back to town?"

Her mom was right.

"Why on earth did you give him Dad's old clothes to wear?" She wasn't sure she felt overly comfortable with this stranger in her dad's clothes. Seeing her dad's clothes folded in the bathroom pricked her grief. She missed her dad and missed the chance of working together with him on the farm.

"Well, it's not like Sam can wear them now, and it's better Blaise has some fresh clothes, his woolen suit stank worse than your clothes. It doesn't hurt to be generous to people, even strangers sometimes."

The kettle boiled, and Claire poured the hot water into mugs. Tea bags bobbed to the surface and the strong English breakfast smell wafted into the room.

Dusty hadn't thought Blaise smelled that bad at all. "He'll be gone tomorrow." *And leave my life for good.*

"You sure you can manage in the shed by yourself? You're nearly asleep at the table." She set down a cup of tea for Dusty.

"No." But there wasn't a choice. She left her half-eaten dinner and took a sip of tea. "I can't think of anyone else to ask for help."

"I think the old Mr. Greg's son, James, is back from Jackarooing up north, I'll give him a ring."

Dusty was about to say no. But her mom was already out of the kitchen to go and make a phone call. Anyway, she knew she needed someone else to help out in the shed, and the reality was she really wanted two other shed hands to ensure no one was being over-worked. But that wasn't about to happen because she couldn't afford it.

She sipped her tea. Blaise was filtering into her thoughts frequently. *If he was free tomorrow, then I'd rather have him in my shed.* A calm flooded outward from her chest. *Yes.* If only she had the guts to ask him. *He had his own work to do, and I've already held him up for one day.* She wasn't interested in a short-term relation-ship, which she was certain that was all he'd be able to offer her. *He looks so out of place in the country.*

Dusty yawned. A holiday sounded like the perfect

excuse to catch up on some sleep and rest. Maybe she'd take her mom's advice and go on one. *Who would look after the farm, though?* She couldn't leave her mom here alone, not that her mom wouldn't be okay here.

Her head pounded.

Dusty rubbed her eyes.

She touched her cheek and flinched. *Aaron.* She was glad that bastard hadn't turned up after what happened last night. She got up and took some paracetamol from the cupboard and swallowed two pills. She sat down and sipped her tea trying to work out when she'd let Aaron into her life and her farm. That wasn't what she'd wanted to do. She just thought he was being a helpful neighbor. *But, of course, not.* She knew better than most what Aaron was really like. Her instincts had always been right about him. *If only I'd listened to them sooner.*

"James will be here at seven thirty tomorrow morning to start working in the shed," said Claire as she came back into the kitchen.

"Thanks." It was a bittersweet result. Someone else who needed to be paid. Another problem, how to pay James, began to build like a stormy cloud in her head.

"Don't worry, Dusty, he'll work well, and we'll get through this. We should have a grain payment coming in next month, and that will help ease things. Plus, I still have some of my savings."

Dusty didn't know how her mom could have savings after over thirty years of living on Acacia

Plains. "Thanks, but keep your savings until things really get bad." She hoped they wouldn't. Wool prices had dropped, and she didn't want to leave nearly thirty bales of wool in the shed sitting there for the rats to nibble on for months hoping the prices would go up. Besides, some money from the sale of the wool would be better than none.

"You're doing a good job running the farm." She rubbed Dusty's back.

"And you're doing a good job helping strange men." Dusty hoped to lighten the mood, but she just didn't have the energy. Her comment came out tighter than she had intended. Her eyes fluttered half closed before she forced them wide open.

"Blaise isn't strange. He's just from the city. I'm sure he could be converted."

"Is that your real plan?" Dusty suspected her mom was trying to do a bit of matchmaking.

"Course not."

"Yeah, right." Dusty got up and hugged her mom. Right now, she didn't care. She was exhausted. "I'm going to bed."

"Without a shower?"

"Too tired." She walked up the hallway quietly so as not to wake Blaise. Tomorrow was another early start, and she had some serious sleeping to do.

Dusty paused at the lounge room door. It was ajar. *I should just go to bed.* She wasn't after anything from him right now. She just wanted to see him, refresh her memory before going to bed. *I've been too hard on him. If he's awake, then I'll apologize.* She hesitated. *Just go in and see. If he's asleep, then leave.* She'd been behaving badly enough toward him for too long. Dusty pushed on the door and went in. She stopped. Her heart pounded.

Blaise lay on the lounge. He snored softly. The sound caused her heart to soften even more toward Blaise. She watched him, dead asleep, exhausted from a hard day's work. Part of her wished he was awake.

He stirred, and she held her breath. His leg hung off the end of the lounge.

Blaise kept sleeping.

Dusty left the room with a new image of Blaise that stirred something she was finding harder and harder to fight.

CHAPTER 11

A STREAM of sunlight woke Blaise. It took a moment for him to remember why he was lying on a lounge in unfamiliar surroundings. His body was sore and stiff, and with strained movements, he rolled off the couch, groaning in pain. He moaned in discomfort as he tried to move. Every muscle in his body burned. Even standing caused him discomfort. Blaise wasn't sure he wanted to be reacquainted with so many muscles in his body all at the same time.

Blaise didn't know what time it was, but the house was hauntingly quiet, and he knew he'd slept in too long. The plan had been to wake early so he could see Dusty again. *Just one more time.* He was sure if he could see her, he'd get up the courage to ask her out. He couldn't get her out of his mind, and he was certain he'd overslept which meant Dusty would be in the shed working already.

I have to see clients. He had to catch up on his work-load today. But he couldn't stop thinking of Dusty and how he could see her one more time. Any other woman, he wouldn't have bothered. Something made him care about Dusty and persist. There was still hope between them. He could sense it. Blaise knew he could convince her to come on a date with him. Desire hardened within him. He took a deep breath. Blaise wanted more than just a date. He wanted to feel the softness of her lips on his, taste her, familiarize himself with her body and feel her toned muscles.

If I want it to happen, I've got to get moving. Already running late, there was no choice for him but to go back into town, so he could buy more appropriate clothes to wear, and he needed to ring clients to reschedule. He went down the hallway into the kitchen.

Claire was fixing the shearers' lunch, chopping a stack of sandwiches into large triangles. "Mornin', sleepy head." Her voice was cheery.

Blaise looked at the clock on the wall, eight forty-five. *Shit, is that the time?* He felt like he'd had a night on the town drinking.

"Morning." Blaise sat down at the table before his legs gave way. "Sorry, I slept in." He felt the need to apologize with Claire preparing food for the shearers and Dusty already out in the shed and him sleeping in. *These women must have been up for hours.* A pang of guilt twisted in his stomach. One day of physical work, and he was walking like an invalid, and yet Dusty was up and working again.

"Eggs?" She put the stack of sandwiches in a Tupperware container, closed the lid, and placed it in the fridge.

"Cereal is fine, I don't want to put you out." Claire's hospitality was warm and generous, but he was thinking he'd overstayed his welcome.

"No trouble. I've got the eggs this morning, and there's plenty. The old girls must be happy." She cleaned away the chopping boards and the bits and pieces of unused tomatoes and lettuce. "Poached, fried, or scrambled?"

The idea of freshly cooked eggs had his mouth watering. "I really should get going. I've got some clients to go and see."

He wasn't about to say he wanted to go to the shed and see Dusty. Right now, that was what dominated his thoughts. He ran his palms down his trousers. *How will Dusty react if she sees me again?*

"Bluey said you could see him this afternoon. Bakers are ready to see you this morning. And the Brown's, who you were meant to see this morning, don't mind if you come tomorrow before you visit the Hay's."

So much for client confidentiality. Blaise wanted to know how Claire managed to do this. "Do you charge for your services?"

Claire laughed. "Don't worry, it was the least I could do. So, your eggs?"

"Poached." Blaise ran his hand through his hair. Dusty stirred a storm in his mind, and he found it hard to think clearly. "What time are the Baker's expecting me?"

He had to get back to town and purchase more appropriate clothing. He surmised he looked a bit clownish right now with the short-legged trousers. Not the image he was going for and not the look that would get him the promotion. *Do I still want that?* He shook his head to settle the thoughts. Of course, he still wanted that. And Dusty. *How would having both work?* A knot tightened in his stomach.

"Nine thirty."

Blaise gasped. There was no way he'd be able to get into town and back again.

"Don't worry, I've cleaned up your suit. It doesn't smell that bad, and at least your shirt and underwear are clean."

Blaise suppressed another gasp. *She's cleaned my underwear too.*

"Don't worry, you've got nothing special." She began cooking two eggs.

That was the first time he'd been told that. *Nothing special.* He squirmed in his seat. He could see where Dusty got her confidence.

"The Baker's won't mind what you look like or what you're wearing as long as you're honest with their books."

Blaise took a deep breath. *I can handle this*. He tried to come to terms with it.

"You've been very generous. I'm beginning to think I'm in debt to you."

"Don't be silly." She slid the eggs on some toast. "I've given you one of Sam's old shirts."

Blaise went to protest, but she put up her hand.

"I've been meaning to pass on some of his clothes, and well, one shirt to you, to help you out, will be a good start," said Claire.

"Thank you." He couldn't believe her generosity to be giving him a shirt, and not just any shirt, her late husband's shirt. He wasn't sure he deserved all of this. The gesture certainly touched his heart and squeezed out plenty of emotion. He blinked quickly.

The phone rang. Claire handed the plate of food to Blaise. "Eat up." She rushed off to answer it.

Blaise breathed deeply, wiped his eyes, and took a mouthful of his eggs. *Delicious*. It was as if his body hadn't been fed for a week. He couldn't believe how hungry he still was.

"Phone's for you." Claire walked back into the kitchen. "First door on the right."

"Who would be ringing me here?" Everyone seemed to know he was here at the Miller's place. "On the landline?" He took out his phone, but he only had one bar for reception.

"Your boss from Adelaide."

Great. Blaise jumped into action and rushed to the phone.

Shit. Even my boss knows exactly where I am.

"Where have you been?" asked Danny.

"Exactly where you've sent me," answered Blaise as he sat down at the office desk. A simple modern desk that had neat piles of paper everywhere. This was the most organized mess he'd ever seen.

"I've been trying to get you all day yesterday. I had clients telling me you were working as a shed hand. I thought you'd lost your mind. In fact, I still think you've lost your mind. I'm not paying you to work in a bloody shed."

Blaise was only half listening to his boss. He lifted up the first page from the nearest pile of papers. He scanned the bank statement and the numbers. Then looked at another sheet of accounting numbers.

"... I think you should come back, now... Blaise? Are you even listening to me?"

"Yes... yes... no... I mean... it's only Wednesday. Two more nights, and I'll be back in Adelaide. I can handle things out here."

Danny groaned. "I don't know, Blaise. You were doing hard, physical labor in a suit? Wearing a bloody tie? I don't think this is good for business. I hate to think about the gossip you've started. Don't get me started on the incident with the sheep."

Blaise swallowed hard. "Gossip was always going to

happen around me. I'm an out-of-towner, even you said that before I left."

"I shouldn't have sent you." Danny grew up in the country, and he understood the life in the rural community.

Blaise kept looking at the notes. Tightness twisted around in his chest. He knew what these numbers meant for Dusty and Claire. Things were tough. "Don't worry, I'm fine."

"You're not. I've heard what you've been wearing to the pub for Christ's sake."

Isn't anything sacred around here?

"It sounds worse than it is," he lied. "Look, you trusted me with this. I'll be back on schedule for visiting clients by tomorrow morning. I'll come back with new figures and a better idea of what the clients want. So, it's going to be a win-win situation."

"Would you bet on that?"

Blaise hesitated. *No, I wouldn't.* "Sure."

"Make sure you don't make things worse." Danny hung up.

Blaise let out a stressed sigh. He was going to do his best to get things back on track. But there was something he wanted to do for Dusty and Claire first if they would let him. The figures he'd just looked through were in his area of expertise, and he knew he could make things a bit better for them if they would let him. It was the least he could do after their hospitality.

He walked out of the office and back to the kitchen. "Claire, I've got an odd proposal."

He couldn't think of an easy way to say this, so he figured he'd take the country approach and just come right out with it. "I can do your books for you... for free, if you like."

Claire's eyes narrowed at him as she stirred a cake mixture. "Now, why would you do that?"

"Same reason you gave me fresh clothes, cooked me dinner, let me sleepover last night, and cooked me breakfast this morning. Never mind about the countless phone calls you made or took to rearrange who I was visiting and when."

Claire didn't say anything. Her lips pursed tight as she mixed the batter.

"I'm good at this. I won't charge, and it can just be a once-off. It could make a difference." He chewed his lip. He never snooped.

"Fine. I have conditions."

"Okay."

"You're not to tell Dusty or anyone else what our situation is."

"Of course. I wouldn't dream of telling anyone else, especially not Dusty."

"The job's yours."

Blaise smiled. It was the way he should've paid them back in the first place instead of playing at being a shed hand. "Give me your files and prepare to be amazed."

Claire smiled. "Don't get my hopes up too much."

"I'm being honest." He glanced at the time on the oven. "I've got to get going."

"Suit's in the bathroom," said Claire. "I'll get the files."

Blaise changed quickly. He wanted to go to the shed and ask Dusty out to dinner. He wrinkled his nose against the lingering lanolin and acidic sheep smell on his suit as he walked out from the bathroom.

He met Claire walking with a large box of files. "Here, let me," said Blaise.

"No, I'm fine."

"I can see where Dusty gets her stubbornness from," said Blaise. He held open the back door for Claire.

"Her father," replied Claire laughing.

At his car, Blaise insisted he take the box of files from Claire. "Thank you." He held out his hand.

"We've gone way beyond that." Claire pulled him into a friendly embrace. "You're almost family."

"I don't know about that," said Blaise.

"Give her time." Claire winked.

"I'll let you know when the files are done," said Blaise.

"I wrote my mobile number on the first page. Don't tell Dusty."

"I won't." He waved as Claire went back to the house. *Now for the hard part.* Blaise walked toward the shed with the intent of convincing Dusty to go on a date with him.

The buzz of the shearing echoed from the shed. *I've come this far.* Blaise walked up the ramp and put his hand on the metal sliding door. I have to try. He knew he wouldn't be satisfied until he asked her. He didn't want it to turn into a regret.

Blaise tensed his arm muscles and pulled open the door.

Dusty looked up from bundling a fleece on the wool table. Sweat beaded on her forehead, strands of her light brown hair had come loose and tumbled down her face. Her eyes were wide with surprise. She looked strong, capable, and he wanted to rush up to her and take her in his arms and kiss her.

Blaise took a deep breath and walked toward Dusty.

"What are you doing here?" asked Dusty.

"I came to see you," Blaise yelled above the noise of the shearing. He stood next to her.

"Why?" Her confused expression caused him to smile.

"Why wouldn't I want to see you?"

She looked gorgeous. Tight jeans, low-cut shirt, and that thunderous stare which sent shivers through his body.

"I've got work to do today," said Dusty. She picked up the fleece, turned and pushed it into the wool baler behind her.

"What about tonight?" He stepped toward her. Dusty concentrated on pushing the fleece down tight.

"Come to dinner with me."

"What?" Dusty spun around and bumped into Blaise.

He grabbed her to stop her from falling. A bolt of desire shot through him. "Dinner, tonight, with me." She fell right in his arms.

"I can't. I've got too much work to do."

"A break would be good."

"Is it a break or a date?"

Blaise detected a hint of softness in her voice. He took a chance. "A date."

Her eyes widened, and she tensed under his grip. He reluctantly released her. "Or a break," he said quickly. "Dusty, I know we haven't started off too well, but I want to get to know you."

"But you'll be off to the city—"

"So? You never know what the future holds."

He couldn't believe what he was saying. Blaise had his future all planned out, and it didn't include living on a farm. "It's dinner. Nothing more."

Her forehead wrinkled as she thought. Blaise held his breath.

"Promise?" Dusty asked.

Blaise nodded. "Promise. I'll even pick you up."

"Not a late night." She pointed her finger at him.

"I know you've got lots of work to do."

"Okay then."

Blaise smiled. "Great. Seven okay?"

"I'll be ready."

"So will I." Blaise winked. He was more than ready now as he looked at Dusty. His body was responding to her, and he struggled to keep himself under control.

"Hey," yelled James sharply. "I could do with some help here."

"Okay, okay." Dusty's cheeks blushed red. Blaise hadn't seen anything so charming that warmed his heart quite so much. There was something between them. He just had to work out how to show Dusty it was there. Then convince himself they could have a future together even though they lived in different worlds.

Dusty watched Blaise leave. His broad shoulders, relaxed walk, tight backside was mesmerizing. She had to focus on shearing, not Blaise. She could smell his musky scent lingering around her. Her stomach suddenly knotted. *I can't date him.*

A fleece fell onto the table, and she began pulling away the soiled wool. Heat from the shed weighed down on the back on her neck. *I don't have the energy to go on a date.* Dusty threw a handful of wool into the wire cage by the shed wall. She swiped away the sweat from her forehead. The knot in her stomach pushed all thoughts of fun aside. But then Blaise filled her thoughts. His endearing smile eased her stress, his blue eyes lightened her heart, and his sexiness stirred a desire within her even though he looked completely out of place wearing a suit in the shed.

"Look out," yelled James.

Dusty stepped back just in time to avoid being collected by the fleece he'd thrown onto the wool table. She clenched her jaw. Now wasn't the time to daydream about Blaise. There was work to do which suddenly didn't feel so burdensome now that she had a date to look forward to tonight.

BLAISE WANDERED down the aisle of the local supermarket, red shopping basket in hand. *I should've asked her what she likes.* He chose two different types of cracker biscuits, water crackers, and wafers, and put them in his basket. So far, he'd made a few executive decisions about what they were going to do tonight for their date, and he hoped Dusty would be happy with what he'd planned. He decided instead of driving back into Wilkton, they could have a picnic on her farm. *I hope she won't mind.*

Blaise walked to the deli and picked out a selection of cheeses, cold meats, olives, semi-dried tomatoes, and dips. He'd managed to make up time today, drop into Wilkton to buy more appropriate clothing to wear, get back to his hotel, shower and shave, and then buy food for his date with Dusty. She'd been in his thoughts all day, and he couldn't wait to see her again tonight. Her long, light brown hair tied up and messy from working, her dirty face and fiery looks had made it difficult for him to crunch numbers with his usual efficiency.

Blaise went through the checkout then wandered next door to the bottle shop. *Red or white?* He decided on both as well as some disposable cups, plates, and cutlery. *That should do it.*

He bundled the bags into the back of his car and then drove out to Acacia Plains. It was nearly seven, and he hoped she'd be finished with her jobs so they could spend time together straight away. While he was happy to lend a hand, it seemed he was only good at making the jobs harder for Dusty.

The car bumped off the sealed road onto the dirt one. Blaise slowed his speed and kept an eye out for the turn-off. He was getting better at distinguishing the roads, but he was still worried about getting lost. There was no way he wanted to even risk getting lost tonight.

Blaise was just about to admit defeat when he saw the road and turned. Up ahead on the horizon he could see Dusty's farm. He grinned proud he had found it. As he drove closer, a knot in his stomach formed. *Will she still want dinner with me after a hard day's work?* Uncertainty knotted inside of him. He didn't know Dusty very well, but he knew she was fighting the connection growing between them. A connection even he couldn't ignore despite him thinking he could live out here.

He drove down the driveway, slowly, in case there were sheep around. He hesitated at the house unsure if Dusty would be inside or if she'd be at the shed. What he did know about her was that she'd be a very hard worker, and in all likelihood, she'd be still working. But he couldn't see her ute anywhere.

Blaise parked by the shed and went inside. "Hello?" he yelled. A few sheep stirred behind the shearing partition. "Dusty?" He walked around the shed but couldn't see her. *Must be at the house.* Nerves fluttered inside his stomach. *She wouldn't stand me up, would she?*

He was about to leave when he heard a vehicle approaching. Blaise walked out onto the small wooden landing. Dusty's ute rattled from the paddock toward the shed. He let out a sigh of relief.

Dusty pulled up next to his car and got out. "Sorry, just finishing the last job. Were you waiting long?"

"Just got here. Hungry?" She looked tired, but there was a brightness about her that made his breath catch in his throat. *She's happy to see me.*

"I could eat a horse." She paused. "I'd better go change first, shower, and put on clean clothes."

Blaise didn't see why. She looked incredibly hot in her work jeans and a shirt. "You look fine."

"Yeah, right. I'm getting cleaned up first." Dusty strolled toward the house. "Where are you taking me?"

"Here." Blaise rushed down the ramp to catch up to

her. He wanted the best for Dusty, and right now, he thought a picnic wouldn't be enough to wow her. She looked quizzically at him.

"I brought us a gourmet picnic. I just need a suggestion where exactly we can eat. Maybe the shearing shed?"

"No way," said Dusty. "I know a good place for a picnic."

"Yeah?" He watched her closely. She didn't seem disappointed with the idea of a picnic at her farm.

Dusty nodded. She kicked off her boots by the back door of the house. "First, I'm having a shower. You can have a cup of tea while you wait. I won't take long."

Blaise followed her inside. He'd never known a woman to be able to get ready quickly.

"Good to see you found more suitable clothes."

Blaise harrumphed. "Suit didn't measure up out here."

Dusty laughed as she walked into the kitchen. "Blaise is here."

"Good to see you again, Blaise," said Claire. She pushed a cake tin into the oven.

"Thanks."

"Can you make him some tea while I get ready?" Dusty didn't wait for an answer and rushed off.

Blaise sat down on a chair at the kitchen table. "I don't want to be any trouble."

"No trouble." Claire wiped her hands on her apron.

"I just made a pot of tea." She poured the tea into two cups. "What are you two up to tonight?"

Blaise flushed red. He couldn't help it. Dusty had been on his mind a lot, and he knew what he wanted to do, but it was too soon. "Picnic," he finally said.

"Good thing it's cooling down outside then." Claire sat opposite to Blaise with a sigh. "Do you need anything?"

"I think I've got everything."

"You're a thoughtful man." Claire sipped her tea.

Blaise reddened under her compliment. Would Dusty think so? "And you're a very generous lady."

"Well now, anything for a man who makes my Dusty happy."

Blaise raised his eyebrow.

"Oh, I noticed." Claire winked.

"I haven't looked at the figures yet," said Blaise quietly.

"All in good time. I know you'll get to them."

"Ready?" Dusty came into the kitchen wearing a light blue summer dress, damp hair tossed into a neat messy look and sandals.

Blaise's jaw dropped. He liked her in her rough work clothes, but this was something else. It was a pleasant, sexy surprise. He crossed his legs and breathed slowly to try and contain his own physical response.

"You look beautiful," said Blaise. He took pleasure

in seeing her cheeks color red. She dropped her head a little.

"Right, you two out of here," said Claire. "I've got baking to do."

Blaise stood up. "Show me where to go." He felt naked allowing her to take control of the date. He'd never done this before.

"You'll like this place," said Dusty. She turned quickly, her dress flowed out around her legs.

"I already do." He clamped his mouth shut. He couldn't flirt like that when her mom was within earshot.

Dusty glanced over her shoulder and smiled. She pushed on the back door and he followed her, not wanting her out of his sight for a moment.

"We'll go in the ute," said Dusty.

"Wouldn't it be more comfortable..." he hesitated not wanting to offend her. His Audi would be more comfortable than her ute.

"Can't take your car out in the paddock. It might start a fire."

"What about your beautiful dress? Won't you get it dirty?" He was about to offer to take it off for her, but managed to stop himself.

"This old thing? We won't be long in the ute."

Once again, without effort, Dusty had undone him. He didn't like not being the one in control, but he didn't fight it. He was on a date with Dusty, and he didn't want to ruin it.

The dogs jumped on the back of the ute as Dusty and Blaise approached.

"Hope you don't mind company," said Dusty.

"Not at all." He got the bags of food from his car. "I can drive."

"I know where to go." She got in leaving Blaise no choice but to get into the passenger's side. He put the food by his feet. *This has got to be the first date where I'm being driven.* He rested his arm on the open window and looked out to the paddocks. So much brown. The wind tousled his hair. A sense of freedom washed over him. Living out here might not be so bad. Then he caught a rotting smell on the breeze and gagged. *Maybe not.*

Dusty laughed. "Doesn't get any fresher out here."

"It's a bit much." She looked alive driving the ute down the paddock.

Suddenly, he realized not only was he not in control, but he had no idea where they were going. When he looked at Dusty, he didn't care. As long as she was with him, they could go wherever. He never thought he'd get this far with Dusty. A part of him thought maybe if he did, then something would happen, and they would go their separate ways, but instead, he was starting to see more of a future with her. This woman had stirred one hell of a dust cloud that he was willing to chase and catch.

～

DUSTY PARKED the ute near a wire fence. "Here we are."

Blaise looked around confused.

"Over there in the old ruins. We can sit there and watch the sun set."

"Perfect." Blaise grinned at her. Her breath caught in her throat. His gaze warmed her, but more than that, his blue eyes connected with hers. Dusty relaxed under his spell. He was surprisingly easy- going, the opposite of how she often was. His smooth red lips, clean-shaven jawline, and spicy scent pulled her toward him. She wanted to taste and touch this delight that sat in her ute.

The dogs jumped off the back of the ute causing it to rock. The spell broke.

"Let's eat," said Dusty. "I'm starving."

She got out quickly before she leaned over and kissed Blaise. *It can't happen.* Dusty walked around the front of the ute. *We're from different worlds.* She knew how heartbroken and grief-stricken she'd feel if she left her farm. *I wouldn't want to impose that on him.*

"Want me to carry anything?" asked Dusty.

Blaise juggled the shopping bags, blanket, and wine. "I've got it, thanks." A bag slipped, and he moved quickly to grab it before it hit the ground.

"Let me take something." Dusty took hold of one of the bags and eased its tangled handles from Blaise's fingers. Her hand brushed over his skin. A bolt of heat shot along her hand and arm, dissipating out into the rest of her body. She paused, savoring the feeling but wanting more.

"Thanks." His voice jolted her back to reality.

Dusty quickly stepped back from him, worried she might start something that could never be finished. Not when he lives in the city. And Blaise looked like he belonged in the bright lights and buzz of the city. He wasn't wearing his sexy suit, but he still looked hot in his new polo shirt, cream shorts, and cheap flip-flops. *A city boy through and through.*

"This way." Dusty took the lead as she was used to doing from managing the farm.

She put the bag on the ground and pushed the top two lengths of the fence wire down. "I'll hold it down and you can step over it." When Blaise didn't step over, she looked up. "Come on, it won't hurt you."

Blaise stood with a shocked expression.

Dusty frowned. "What's wrong?"

"I'm... well..." he sighed. "I should be the one holding the fence for you."

"Why?" Dusty had a defensive tone in her voice.

"You're wearing a dress for a start."

Dusty sighed heavily with annoyance. Then leaned forward, pushed down on the wires of the fence, kicked out her leg back over the fence, then the other. She let go of the wire, and it bounced up and down as she stood triumphantly on the other side of the fence.

Blaise's eyes widened.

"A farm girl knows how to get over a fence without flashing her knickers." She picked up the bag of food.

"I can see that."

Dusty detected a hint of disappointment. She grinned to herself as she walked toward the ruins, swinging her hips deliberately.

"Wait up," yelled Blaise.

Dusty glanced over her shoulder to see Blaise awkwardly trying to get over the fence while still holding out the shopping bags. She held her breath, and by some miracle, he made it over the fence, stumbling a little to regain his balance.

"Easy, huh," she said.

"Only if you're wearing a skirt," said Blaise. He nearly tripped on a rock.

"Careful." Dusty ran to catch his arm and help him.

"I'm all right."

"Glad you're fine, city boy. I think you need more practice climbing fences." Dusty felt his arm muscles and let her touch linger.

Dusty let her hand drop away from his arm. His strength left her hand tingling. "Hang around long enough, and I just might teach you. I promise I'll go easy on you." It had been tough managing the farm after her dad died, keeping men in line and doing physical work every day had caused many tears to be shed in private. Not so much these days because she'd toughened up. But she couldn't help feeling she could toughen up more.

"... a good sport."

Dusty realized she'd tuned out. Guilt pricked at her stomach. Blaise was fun to be around. Even if it would only be for a few days, she wanted to give him her full attention.

"What used to be here?" asked Blaise.

Dusty spread out the blanket in front of the partly fallen stone wall. "This is where my grandfather went to school, along with other kids from surrounding farms." Dusty kicked off her sandals and sat on the blanket.

Blaise took out the gourmet foods he'd brought. "Didn't know if you liked red or white."

"Both. Let's start with the white since it's warm."

"Sav blanc okay?"

"Sure."

The dogs came to say hello, and Dusty firmly pushed them away. They reluctantly sat at the edge of the blanket, brown eyes pleading for treats.

"None for you," said Dusty firmly.

"I don't" know, you think we could eat all this?" asked Blaise.

"I'm hungry," said Dusty.

"I don't know how you keep going." Blaise opened the lid of the avocado dip.

"What do you mean?"

"All that physical work every day in the shed." He started assembling the plastic wine glasses.

Dusty shrugged her shoulders. "I love it."

"I can see that." He poured the wine and handed her a glass.

"I couldn't think of doing anything else. I'd feel lost not living here." Dusty held the glass of wine.

"I can't imagine what that would be like."

"No?" Dusty looked at Blaise. He shook his head and looked out to the horizon where the sun was sinking. "You don't feel that way about the city?"

"Not the same way you feel about here. I love the city. But this..." he swept out his hand, "... I dunno. This is something worth connecting to."

"It sure is." She raised her glass. "Here's to the land."

"And to new friends," said Blaise, clinking his plastic glass against hers.

"It's a good drop," said Dusty. She leaned back on the blanket and spread her legs out in front of her.

"Glad you like my taste in wine."

Dusty felt heat blush on her cheeks. Blaise had such a powerful effect on her. He was evoking some strong emotions inside her, and she struggled to keep a lid on them. She sighed and looked out over her land. It was flat cropping land with groups of eucalyptus trees lining the roads. Sheep talked to each other in nearby paddocks, birds tweeted in the trees, and the temperature cooled.

"I'm in heaven," said Dusty.

"Me, too."

Dusty glanced at Blaise and caught him looking

at her. He wasn't taking in the landscape like she'd been. Heat flared through her body. She quickly looked away. Dusty squeezed her legs together and wriggled her toes to try and release the sexual tension that was building in her. She could feel him staring at her. Her previous 'I can't do this' was rapidly changing into I can do this with him. She swallowed a large gulp of wine to distract herself then leaned forward and took a piece of salami. "This spread is great. Thank you."

Blaise's smile reached his eyes, and Dusty's heart softened more.

"You're welcome," said Blaise.

"Could you ever live here?" asked Dusty.

"I never thought about it."

Dusty felt a restriction around her chest. Her heart hardened a little. *I can't take a chance with him. He wouldn't like it here. He wouldn't last long.*

"I think in the right circumstances I could."

"Like what?" It was hard to read his face in the gray light of dusk.

"You tell me." He inched closer.

Dusty didn't move. Her pulse sped up, and her mouth dried. A dusty storm of emotions let loose inside her. She wanted to take things further with Blaise, but she was painfully aware he was leaving in a few days. *Out of sight, out of mind.* Suddenly, the day's work caught up with her. She suppressed a yawn.

"Sorry." She saw his shoulders slump.

"I'll take you home. You need to sleep because I know you have another day of tough work ahead."

"Thank you."

He'd always been nothing but polite and gentleman-like to her. Dusty liked that. It made a refreshing change to the battle she'd had with Aaron.

He helped her up. His hands brushed the skin on her shoulders. Shivers rippled through her speaking to her about the potential with him if only she was brave enough to let go.

CHAPTER 12

BLAISE DROVE BACK into town for a pub meal, back to Ol' Billies. It was dark, and he was tired from the long day but content with how he was now adapting to country life. He caught up on seeing clients today, and thanks to the mud map Claire drew for him, he'd only gotten lost once. Not a bad effort since he'd gone to three different places.

The date last night with Dusty gave him a boost in confidence. He was going to see her tonight at Ol' Billies.

All day he couldn't get her out of his mind. But there was more. There were other thoughts making his head ache.

What about the junior partnership? It was what he strove for in his work, it was what kept him going when numbers didn't add up or clients were difficult to work with. It was his motivation and plan for the future.

Now he wasn't so sure that was what he wanted. He saw how in love with the land Dusty was, and he knew in the city he missed this connection. Blaise was beginning to think maybe he wanted to have that sort of connection in his life.

Could I start up my own business here? Some of the people he'd met in Wilkton had offered him their business accounts to do. *At least I'm leaving some good impression here after my blundering start.* He had a solid reputation as an accountant. *Could I really live in the county?* He was used to certain luxuries, a certain lifestyle, which certainly wasn't out here. *Could I?*

He groaned as his mind whirled around with the thoughts. All he cared about was seeing Dusty tonight.

Dressed in long cargo shorts and a RM Williams polo top, Blaise felt more relaxed as he parked his car and walked to Ol' Billies pub. There hadn't been a lot of options in terms of color and cuts and even sizes. He basically got what fit him that wasn't in a pinkish color. He'd dropped his suits off at the dry cleaners and nearly died from the stink. I could never get use to the smell. The lady behind the counter wrinkled her nose. "What have you been doing?" she'd asked.

"Becoming a local," he had answered. That was what he'd certainly been doing today. A bit of light banter with the dry-cleaning lady resulted in her handing over her books for him to go through. He was tempted not to mention this to his boss for now. If he could convince Beryl he could do the motel's books and a few others, then he'd definitely get that junior partnership and make up for all the gossip he started. Then he would only be a step away of owning part of the business. *Could I start up my own business?* The mixed thoughts tumbled over each other in his mind.

Beryl gave him a ribbing for not coming home the night before, so much so he thought he was a naughty teenager who had done something very wrong instead of being plain exhausted and basically passed out on the Miller's lounge. Beryl took some convincing, but she eventually took his word for it. Apparently, Beryl was concerned he was taking advantage of the local girls. From what he'd seen of the local girls, they could look after themselves.

"Usual?" asked Kate as he walked into the pub.

"Thanks." Blaise sat down at a table that was more central. A quick glance around the pub revealed that Dusty wasn't there yet. *I'm early*. His heart thudded nervously. He'd never been so undone like this with a woman before. He didn't think she'd stand him up, but he never really knew what Dusty would do. *She's her own dust storm.*

Kate came over with a pint of beer. "You're just in time, the kitchen is about to close, but I convinced the chef to cook you up a beef schnitzel and chips."

"Thanks." Blaise decided to give Kate a tip for being so helpful. He couldn't shake the idea she was angling for a different sort of tip. He wasn't about to give into any primal desires. Besides, there was only one woman he couldn't get out of his head right now, and that was more than enough for him to handle.

He planned to have a few hours off from work in the pub, meet up with Dusty, get to know some of the locals, and then head back to the hotel and get Dusty's books organized so he could hand them back Friday before going back to Adelaide. Unless, of course, things went differently with Dusty, then maybe they would be spending the night together.

Blaise took a sip of his beer. The malty coolness refreshed him after the long day. His muscles were just as sore as they were in the morning, but the beer helped him to forget about the ache, especially in his upper arms.

His stomach grumbled. He'd skipped lunch today mainly because at each place, he'd been given tea and cake and wasn't that hungry. But now he wanted a proper meal.

"Well, look what the cat dragged in." Aaron sat down opposite him.

Blaise hadn't managed to go through Aaron's books yet to do the final number crunching. That was going to be tomorrow's job, after he visited a few more clients.

"Aaron. Did you want to go over figures?"

"No, no, we can do that later." He paused. "That's if you aren't too busy with the locals."

There was tension between them. Blaise had an uneasy feeling something was going on here that he had no idea about. He'd seen the bruise on Dusty's face, but he wasn't sure if it was Aaron's work or a farming mishap. He didn't want to ruin things with Dusty by asking. Things were delicate enough between them. It was a big thing to have had a date last night, and then to meet up at the pub tonight was a great outcome.

He was also nervous Dusty would put up her walls and shut him out if he pushed too hard. Blaise wouldn't have thought Aaron capable of hitting someone until the other night at the pub when he saw a dark side of him, a side he didn't want to see again. He wished Aaron hadn't sat down. All he wanted to do was to meet Dusty in peace. He wasn't so sure this plan was going to work out as simply as he'd hoped now.

"I've got a few clients to visit around here if that's what you're talking about."

Blaise took another sip of his beer. He tensed. *Aaron's a client, be polite.* The reminder to himself sounded hollow.

"That's not what I'm talking about."

Blaise resisted the urge to be rude. Aaron was on edge again over something that he didn't want to be part of. "I have no idea what you're referring to."

"Sure, you do." Aaron glared at him. His eyes were dark with anger and the veins on his neck pulsed.

"No, Aaron I don't. I'm here to meet Dusty and share a meal together."

"Exactly, but it's not just a meal you two have been sharing, is it?"

"Are you going to tell me what the hell you're talking about?" Blaise's blood pressure began to rise. He struggled to keep his cool with Aaron. What he did with Dusty was no one else's business.

"You spent the night with her."

Bloody hell, what rumors are going around about me? Then the pieces began to fall together about what Aaron was talking about. Of course, he'd have a thing for Dusty, he could imagine a few of the men out here would. She was beautiful, strong, and had her own farm. He wasn't about to play easy with Aaron.

"What business is it of yours?" Nothing had happened between Dusty and him, but even that was none of this prick's business.

"She's not available." The veins on Aaron's neck stood out even more, and he clenched his hands into fists.

"What, are you two an item?"

"Something like that."

"So, you'll be finding the guy who punched her then and making sure he doesn't hurt her again?" Blaise barely finished his sentence before Aaron stood up, leaned over in one quick movement, and pushed Blaise on the shoulder, sharp and strong, knocking him back on his chair.

Blaise fell and lay there on the floor stunned for a moment before he got up, his own anger becoming more apparent. Aaron's response confirmed what he thought. *This guy was a tool, a prick, and an asshole.* Client or not, he wasn't going to be pushed around by him.

"Dusty didn't give me the impression that she wasn't available," said Blaise. He wasn't holding back now. He saw Aaron's right punch coming, blocked it, and then landed his right fist in the guy's face with a sickening thud.

Aaron wasn't going to be put off that easy. He recovered and swung another punch toward Blaise. This time his fist met the target, and Blaise's head snapped back, his cheek exploding in pain.

The fight was on. Blaise couldn't see anything else. It was as if the pub surroundings faded into blackness, and there was a spotlight on Aaron as he swung his fists toward the man.

"Break it up, fellas," someone yelled.

Blaise didn't stop, not when there were still punches coming toward him.

Someone grabbed his shoulders and pulled him back. "That's enough."

Blaise protested by struggling to go forward so that he could land one last punch on Aaron's face. But whoever held him, stopped him. He noticed two guys were holding onto Aaron.

"Both of you stop," someone growled at them.

Blaise felt the red anger inside him begin to fade while pain stung his knuckles and face. He tried to shrug off the guys who were holding him, but they held him too tightly.

"Come on, you can go home," said the man with authority. He grabbed Aaron by the scruff and hauled him outside.

"He started it. I'm just here for the beer, George."

"You're both are dickheads, and you're both are getting the fuck out of here. I don't want this shit ruining what should be a peaceful evening for folks after a hard day's work." With the help of two other guys, they dragged Aaron toward the door.

"Yeah, well, you shouldn't let in outsiders." He twisted back to glare at Blaise, but George just pushed him forward making him stumble out of the swinging door.

Blaise shrugged out of the grip of the guys who held him. "I'm fine, I'm fine."

They let him go. His body buzzed from the leftover adrenaline pulsing in his bloodstream. He stumbled and sat on the nearest chair. His vision blurred a little as he tried to process what had just happened.

He looked around the pub wondering what might come next from these people. After all, he'd just picked a fight with their friend. The men let him be. That suited Blaise just fine. No comments, nothing. He wiped his nose. A trail of blood smeared on his hand. He wasn't surprised. His nose felt like it could even have been broken. He blinked through the pain. Blood dripped down on his new polo top. *Dammit.*

"You're hurt," said Nat. She handed him a bunch of paper towels.

Just when he thought he was getting the hang of life out here in the country, things had to go wrong again. This wasn't going to be an easy one to explain away to Danny. Blaise held the bunched- up paper towels to his nose and leaned forward.

"Right, when ya can drive, ya can get out of here too," said George as he returned. "It would be best if ya don't ever come back 'ere."

Always wanted to be banned from a pub, Blaise thought hysterically. Nat put down his meal on the table. Eating was the last thing he wanted to do now.

"Fine by me," he said. He was more than happy to leave, return to Adelaide, and never come back.

CHAPTER 13

Dusty closed the shearing door at the end of another day of hard work. Her entire body was sore and tired, yet strength rippled through her muscles, and a sense of satisfaction at coming one step closer to finishing the shearing for another year.

Molly jumped up, her dusty paws resting on the top of Dusty's jeans.

"Good girl." She patted the dog. Then Ted came up wanting attention. "All right, boy, come here."

Dusty let him jump up on her, something she didn't normally do as she rubbed them both behind the ears.

Her phone vibrated in her pocket. "Down you get." She pulled it out. There was a message from Bell.

Dinner tonight? xo

DUSTY TYPED A QUICK REPLY.

Already booked up tonight.

SHE DIDN'T WANT to be talking too much about Blaise. Not when she had no idea where this was going to lead. *I should've said no to dinner tonight at the pub.* She'd been tired last night, but also refreshed from spending time with Blaise, and the thought of not seeing him again scared her. So, when he asked, she said yes without thinking.

Dusty walked down the ramp from the shearing shed. Her shoulders ached, her legs were numb, and her head pounded demanding a decent sleep. She'd finished the work with the sheep, but she needed to feed the dogs, collect the eggs, and then she planned to drop in front of the television and sleep until tomorrow. *Just one more day.*

What?! Who? Aaron?

. . .

THE RESPONSE from Bell caused a twist of guilt in Dusty's stomach. She'd been too busy to catch up with her school friend and fill her in on certain details that had happened. She wiped the sweat from her forehead. So much had happened in only a few days she didn't even know where to start now.

> I un-best friend you!

CAME the next message when Dusty hadn't replied. Dusty smiled.

> City boy. Blaise. Talk later.

SHE WENT DOWN toward the chook shed, the dogs following at her heels. She had to get a move on if she wanted to meet up with Blaise tonight. *How could it ever work out with him?*

You better!

SHE ONLY HAD to feed the chooks and dogs then get ready which would take all of ten minutes max, which was good because right now, she should be driving into Wilkton to meet Blaise. Her body responded with a flush of lustful heat as she thought about Blaise. He had been such a gentleman last night. He knew she was tired and simply took her home without pushing himself on her. *Aaron would've.* A tightness gripped her throat. Blaise caused such a different response. *Aaron's not for me.* She pushed Aaron out of her mind. All day she'd amused herself with pleasant thoughts about Blaise. That's what she wanted. A man who treated her with respect. A man she could trust. Her heart sunk. A man who lived close by, not two hundred miles away.

Enjoy yourself!

DUSTY READ the text from Bell. *I will.* She put her phone away. She quickened her pace and looked at the dogs. "Looks like I'd better hurry."

Dusty got ready in record time and then drove her ute into Wilkton. *What am I doing? What do I want with him?* She knew she didn't want to take things further with Blaise. Well, she did, but he'd be gone tomorrow, and she wasn't the sort of girl who engaged in short relationships. Just being with Blaise was fun. There was more between them. She could feel it. It thrilled and scared her both at once.

Up ahead she saw Aaron's ute. Her chest restricted. *He's traveling too fast.* He wasn't slowing down. Dusty gripped the steering wheel tight. *Will he hit me?* He went by, the whoosh of the air rattled her ute and her. *What's wrong with him?* She checked in her rearview mirror. Aaron kept going. She let out a sigh of relief. For a moment, she was worried he'd stop and want to talk to her. She didn't want anything to do with Aaron anymore. That, she was certain about. *But what about Blaise?* He was a city boy and totally clueless about her life. *What to do with him?* Her cheeks burned hot. She knew exactly what to do with him. And that's the thought she held in her mind as she parked her ute and walked into the pub.

Immediately she knew something had happened. A table was overturned and so were some chairs. *Damn, I missed the fight.* She looked around for Blaise. There were two older men casually drinking at the bar as if nothing had happened. She froze. He sat on a chair with an ice pack over his eye. Blood splattered around the color of his shirt.

"What happened?" She rushed over to him and knelt beside him.

"It's nothing," he answered.

"It doesn't look like nothing." Dusty kneeled down next to him and tried to look under the ice pack, but Blaise refused to let her.

"Who did this to you?" She chewed her bottom lip. She knew who.

"Aaron seemed to think I was muscling in on his territory." Blaise looked at her, his blue eyes reflecting hurt which squeezed at her heart.

"Well, you aren't." She clenched her fists. "I'm going to break his bloody balls for doing this."

"No, you're not," said Blaise calmly.

"Yeah, well, he doesn't own me. No one does."

Blaise smiled.

"What's funny?" Anger burned through her. She was going to teach Aaron a thing or two for messing around with her life.

"This isn't funny at all."

"No, it's not." Blaise continued to smile.

Dusty tilted her head to the side questioningly at Blaise.

"No one could ever own you. Why would they want to? You're perfect as you are."

Dusty's jaw dropped, and her heart paused as his words sunk in. She had no idea what to say. Unusual, as she always knew what to say.

Blaise laughed. "I'm feeling much better now. How about we eat?" He took the ice pack off his face. "We just have to go somewhere else, I've been kicked out of here."

"Oh my God." Dusty's eyes widened at the purple hues around Blaise's eye.

"That bad?"

"Well... no..."

"Don't worry. I've always wanted to be kicked out of a pub."

"Yeah, well, I feel responsible."

Blaise placed his hand on her arm. "Dusty, don't you ever blame yourself for Aaron's actions." The tone of his voice made her shiver. "Promise."

Dusty chewed the bottom of her lip. Her cheek ached from where Aaron hit her. Emotions welled inside of her. Her eyes watered, but she fought them down.

"Dusty," he spoke gently. "This isn't your fault."

His voice broke the lid on her emotions. The fear of being hit and being scared spilled silently down her cheeks. Dusty couldn't push them back anymore. She looked at Blaise and knew it could've easily been her sitting there with an ice pack on her face.

"I'm sorry," she whispered. "I don't know what has come over me." Now that the tears came, she couldn't stop them.

Blaise didn't say anything. He took her in his arms. She rested her head on his shoulder and sobbed quietly letting out the emotions she'd tried so hard to keep away and stop herself from feeling. She allowed his strong arms to wrap around her, holding her, and keeping her protected. The tears flowed until there was no more emotion, and Dusty pulled away.

"I'm sorry." She rummaged through her handbag for a tissue.

"Don't be." Blaise spoke softly. "He hit you, didn't he?"

Suddenly the emotion was there again and more tears cascaded down her cheeks. She nodded. It was true, and she promised herself never to deny it. It was so much harder to admit what had happened than she realized.

"Bastard."

"Yeah." She sniffled, dabbing her eyes with a tissue. "I'll be okay."

"I know you will."

His confidence in her stilled her emotions. "I'll just go wash my face."

He nodded.

Dusty went to the bathroom and splashed water on her face. She looked in the mirror. The bruise was nearly gone. Aaron had done the same to Blaise. It caused knots to form in her stomach. Even though Blaise told her not to blame herself, she did. She splashed more water on her face to cool her eyes. They were red and puffy. There was no way she wanted to go on a date now. She dried her face and went back to tell Blaise she needed to go home. But when she saw him sitting patiently at a table with a glass of water, she knew the only person she wanted to be with right now was him. Especially, when he looked up and smiled gently at her.

Dusty took a deep breath. "I'm not really hungry, but do you want to get a drink?"

"I hear the Italian place is good." He stood up.

"It's more than good." They walked to the door. "It also has good wine and some sharing plates."

"Lead the way." Blaise held open the door.

Despite what happened, Dusty smiled. It felt good to be with Blaise. More than good. All the bad stuff seemed to fade away when he was with her. All her cares and worries blew away as she walked next to him down the street.

For the next three hours, they nibbled on a shared plate and drank wine talking about their separate lives.

Dusty enjoyed hearing about what he got up to in the city and was pleasantly surprised when Blaise showed a genuine interest in her life on the farm. All too soon the restaurant closed, and they were forced out. Dusty felt a different person now as she left with Blaise. *He certainly brings out my better side.*

"I'm going to have a lot of explaining to do when meeting clients tomorrow," said Blaise as they walked down the dark street.

"Don't worry, they'll know who did it and won't ask."

"True." Blaise smiled. "I'd forgotten about the grapevine."

"Don't ever forget about it, it always works."

"Thanks for a great night," said Blaise. He turned and paused. "Are you all right?" The concern in his voice melted her heart. Her eyes watered, but she pushed the tears back.

"I am," she whispered. "Thank you."

He picked up her hands and squeezed them tight. She felt her knees weaken from his touch. She wanted more, but now, after what had happened tonight, she was an emotional mess and didn't want to complicate things any more than they already were. Somehow, she knew by looking into his blue eyes which were full of concern, that Blaise knew this too.

"I want to see you again," he answered.

"Me, too." Dusty said the words without thinking.

"I'll stay the weekend. Maybe I can see you tomorrow?"

"I'd like that." She didn't care about the future. Just now. And right now, she wanted to see him again. Her answer was rewarded with a huge smile from Blaise.

"Thank you." He leaned forward and brushed his lips on her cheek. The soft touch sent tiny sparks rippling through her body. There was no way she was going to be able to resist him. He didn't do anymore. He led her to her ute.

"I look forward to seeing you tomorrow night."

"Me, too." She got in and started the ute. She didn't want to leave him, but he stepped back onto the curb and waved. She reversed, waved back, and began counting down when she could see him again.

CHAPTER 14

"A client, a fuckin' client. You hit a client!" Danny yelled at Blaise through the phone.

Blaise kissed goodbye the last chance of getting the junior partnership. Now, he hoped he'd keep his job. His jaw hurt. Date number two with Dusty went well. It wasn't what he'd expected, but the pain in his nose and eye faded when he thought of her and how strong she'd been last night. *It took guts to stay and finish a date after what had happened.*

The good thing about being in the country was the lack of phone reception, and it meant that it was nearly twenty-four hours later when he was back in town looking for somewhere to eat, before his boss managed to contact him.

"What were you thinking?" Danny wasn't calming down.

Blaise squirmed in the seat of his car. He'd just

parked to pick up his dry cleaning when his phone rang.

"That I didn't want to be beaten to a pulp." He hadn't gone there looking for a fight, though he suspected Aaron had. He'd visited some clients today. They all knew how he got his black eye and why his nose was swollen. They didn't want to get involved and so he just got on with completing the accounts.

"Yeah, well, great work, now we've lost a client. One of our bigger clients, too."

Blaise was sort of expecting something like this to happen but had been hoping like hell it wouldn't.

Danny wasn't exactly sympathetic toward his plight which frustrated Blaise as he clenched his fist. "Aren't you even worried about your own employee?"

Blaise had been talking all day, and all he wanted to do was to be quiet so his jaw could rest. He thought he probably should put some more ice on it.

"Not when I've been told you started a fight."

With a twist in his gut, Blaise realized what his silence and avoidance of not contacting his boss might have cost him. Of course, Aaron would ring his boss and say he started the fight.

Blaise put his hand on his head. It was like being here in the country had fried his brain. "Well, maybe you better get down here and talk to the locals and find out what really happened."

"I just might have to."

"I thought you knew me better than to know I'd lie

to you, and I wouldn't fight, unless someone else forced me to."

"It's not what I've heard. I shouldn't have let you go on this trip. Look at the mess you've made."

"You shouldn't listen to just one person, and especially not Aaron. I've caught up with the workload, the clients I saw were happy today. It's going well."

"Do you really need me to remind you that you hit a client?"

Blaise kept quiet. He wasn't about to get anywhere with his boss yelling down the phone at him. "I'll be back—"

"Don't think that this is over." Danny hung up.

Blaise let out a string of swear words. His job was on the line, big time. *Maybe I should think of starting my own business?* It wasn't the first time he'd thought that today. Something happened to him last night when he was hit. It was more than that. He was there to support Dusty, and they connected further. Much more deeply than he thought possible in such a short time. There was no way he wanted to leave her. He remembered the accounts. With a sinking heart, he knew she'd go ballistic if she found out. *I can't let her find out then.* It was a favor to her and Claire.

Blaise went in and collected his suit. It felt odd looking at it as if it was something he never wanted to wear again. He quite liked visiting clients in smarter casual clothes. *Maybe I can get used to this life?*

He drove out of Wilkton toward Dusty's farm. His

thoughts turning over about his future faded the closer he got to Acacia Plains. She was definitely dominating his thoughts.

His gut instinct told him he was not only out of the running for the partnership, but that he no longer had a job. As soon as he walked back into the office, he'd be asked to pack his desk then escorted out. One thing he was sure of, he was glad he punched Aaron, and he was also glad he came to the country. He wouldn't change that part at all. Now, he just needed to step up and start his own business and see if chasing Dusty would lead to them dating. That was why he was out here in the middle of nowhere because he had to see Dusty.

Blaise saw a farm on the left come into view as he drove along the dirt road. He smiled feeling pleased he hadn't actually gotten lost. The real hurdle was going to be how receptive Dusty would be to his unannounced arrival.

He turned into the driveway at Acacia Plains. He kept going straight ahead to the shearing shed where he saw her ute parked.

Molly ran out to greet him. "Hey, Molly," he said to her through the opened window while he parked next to Dusty's ute. She wagged her tail. He got out and gave her a pat. Ted only lifted his head up from the ute to see who arrived and then went back to sleep.

"Been working hard, boy." Ted answered with a noisy yawn.

It was unusually quiet. Then Blaise realized there was no sound from the shearing. Must have finished early. He hoped so because then maybe he could get Dusty off the farm for a break.

Small dust clouds blew up from the ground, swirled around, then fell back to earth. *That's how she makes me feel.* Blaise walked up the ramp into the shed and went through the door. He saw Dusty straight away. He stood and watched at her work. She was kneeling down in front of a bale of wool that looked like it was about to burst. A stencil in her left hand and a roller in the other, she was inking the bales of wool with the words, Acacia Plains. She looked less tired, more relaxed. She looked hot as hell. There were some fleeces lying on the floor ready to be packed away and some loose wool here and there. The shed almost felt empty without the buzz of the shears and the sound of hooves on the wooden grating. He didn't care. Finally, he got to see her again, and with how his body stirred, he knew he wanted more between them.

"Hi, Dusty."

DUSTY TURNED SHARPLY at the sound of her name. She hadn't heard anyone drive in and come into the shearing shed. Normally, the dogs would've barked at a visitor. She looked at Blaise. *What's he doing here?* Her heart quickened.

"Don't tell me you're lost again?" She composed herself quickly, on the outside. Inside her, a lustful heat had begun to build just from the sight of Blaise.

"No." Blaise smiled. "You're keen working on a Saturday."

"Farm jobs aren't aware of the weekend." She shrugged her shoulders.

"Want some help?" He walked over to her. With every step closer, the heat inside her intensified and her thigh muscles clenched in anticipation. He took the stencil from her hand and repositioned it on the front of the bale, lining it up with the letters she had already marked with ink.

"Is this right?"

She was almost disappointed he didn't kiss her there and then. *Of course, he wouldn't do that.* She looked at him. He was a gentleman. "Yes. Look, you're a natural."

Dusty tried to calm down as her pulse raced. She could feel his heat embrace her, and she found herself wanting more, wanting to be enveloped in his arms. "Make sure you hold it still."

"An archaic method for such modern times," said Blaise.

His gentle voice sent shivers along her spine.

"It works." She began rolling the ink over the stencil, pushing hard to get the ink into the hessian material, trying to use it as a distraction.

Dusty's face flushed. "I'm glad you came by." She finished inking the letters.

Blaise removed the metal stencil. The words, Acacia Plains, curved at the top of the bale. "Is that all?" asked Blaise.

"The words have to go on top of the bale, and then on the other side. Plus, there's these stencils to put on, my wool classer's number and the type of wool in the bale."

"That's a lot of stenciling." Blaise picked up one of the stencils. "AAA, now this must be top quality wool."

"Yes. It goes here." She pointed to the bottom part of the bale.

Blaise knelt down next to her to hold the stencil in position. His body brushed against hers sending a ripple of heat through her. Dusty held her breath as the waves of heat flooded her body again and again. She couldn't concentrate properly. The roller went over his fingers, leaving black tire-like marks.

"Oi," he said.

"Sorry." She grinned and rolled over his fingers again.

"I hope this comes off."

"Umm..." She looked at him innocently.

"It better come off."

"It will." She didn't mention that it might take a week.

He narrowed his eyes at her. Then ran the back of his fingers on her arm, leaving a trail of black ink.

"Hey, that's not fair."

"Apparently, it will come off," he said teasingly. "So, there's no problem."

"This means war," she said and moved the roller on his arm, leaving a black blotch.

"No fair." He tried to grab her, but she was quicker. She stepped away. "Come back here."

Dusty couldn't help laughing, which was her downfall, because when he stood, she only managed to take two steps before he grabbed her around the waist. "Tell me, does it come off?"

"Lots of things will come off... in time," she teased.

"Is that right?"

She was laughing too hard to answer. He moved her around to face him. There was a glint of happiness in his eyes, but there was more. The longer she looked into his blue eyes, the more his mood changed to a passionate shine. His arms pinned her in strong and tight, but she knew if she wanted to, she could get away. She didn't want to get out of his hold.

He smelled spicy and fresh. His scent intoxicated her. All she wanted to do was to kiss him.

She held his glance as he leaned forward. A burst of pleasant heat exploded on her lips as they met. The sensation rippled through her body right down to her toes. She moved her lips with his increasing the heat between them. Their tongues brushed, and she eased further into the kiss with him, pushing them together.

The kiss ended naturally, they separated looking at each other.

"Is that the real reason you came over?" she asked.

"No... I mean..."

Dusty took pleasure at seeing his face redden. She wriggled out of his embrace laughing, picked up some loose wool, and threw it at him.

"I'm not easy, you know," she teased.

He was too slow to get out of the way and the wool landed in his hair. "I know." He smiled. "Come here."

"You..."

But he was much quicker than she'd expected, and before she could make him chase her, they were kissing once more. Dusty sighed with pleasure as her breasts pushed into his chest. She could feel his strength, taste it too, as she kissed him and wanted more.

Blaise moved his hands along her waist finding the edge of her shirt, slipping underneath and gliding along the smooth skin of her back. She kept her lips on his as his hands ran along her back, his fingers just touching her skin. Electric shivers sparked all over her body.

She slipped her hands under his T-shirt. His chest muscles were smooth and a delight to feel under her fingertips. She moved her hands back down and then lifted his shirt, tugging it upward. He reluctantly broke the kiss and helped her remove his T-shirt. A delight of toned muscles greeted her, but only for a moment before he pulled her into him and kissed her again, urgently.

Dusty ran her hands over his skin until it bumped from her touch. In search for new areas to explore, she moved her hands down his back as far as she could reach until meeting the top of his jeans. He pulled her tighter against him, and she felt him harden. She tried to go slow, but an urgency took over.

She slipped her hand to his groin. He pulsed under her touch. Blaise began unbuttoning her shirt, his fingers brushing on her exposed skin, setting her on fire. He pushed the shirt over her shoulders. The material tickled her skin as it fell to the ground.

Blaise kissed along her neck, his hands on her lower back holding her tight. Intoxicated from his touch, she held onto his waist, leaning backward giving him full access as his kisses moved further down her chest toward the top of her breasts. He followed the outline of her bra causing her to groan with pleasure.

He moved his hand to her breast and squeezed gently but firmly causing her nipples to harden. He pinched one softly, then slipped his fingers under the top of her bra cup, moving away the lace and exposing her breast. He rolled her nipple between his fingers, and she groaned, lifting her leg up around his waist. More heat flooded through her body.

Gently, he put her breast in his mouth and played on her nipple with his tongue. She arched backward again, losing control with him. She groaned every time he put a little pressure on her nipple.

He kissed his way back up to her mouth, and she was eager to taste him again and to feel the softness of his lips against her. When their lips met, her body relaxed into his embrace as she surrendered to the act. He held her tight against him, his erection firm against her through his jeans, giving her a hint of what was still to come.

His hands slipped up to the hooks of her bra, and after a little tugging and pulling, he unhooked it and pushed it away. He cupped her breasts and ran his thumb over her hardened nipples, her thigh muscles contracting with each touch. The moisture gathered between her legs with each touch.

He lowered her to the floor, on to the wool, and positioned himself next to her, slipping his hands down her waist to the top of her jeans. He teased her by slipping his fingers just under the denim but not going any further. She groaned in frustration and lifted up her hips, enjoying the tension between them. Gracefully and quickly, he then unzipped her jeans. Wanting more, she helped by wriggling out of them and kicking off her boots. He ran his hands up both of her legs as she lay back down in the wool. He slipped his fingers under her knickers, her legs parting naturally. He followed the edge of her knickers, slipping his fingers under the material, and out again, in and out, sending waves of heat rippling through her body causing her breath to quicken and her back to arch each time.

Dusty relaxed into the sensation. She'd never had this much attention before, and it was thrilling and nerve-wracking, but she knew all she could do was to go with the flood of pleasure he sent running through her entire body. He slipped off her knickers, and with a hand on her hip, reached up and kissed her on the mouth. This time when he touched her, it wasn't just on the surface. He slipped his fingers into her moisture, between her folds, dipping inside then slowly moving toward her tight bud. She groaned. His fingers glided in slow circles along the area. He'd found her spot, and her sounds encouraged him to move quicker and firmer as the pleasure rippled through her body driving her toward bursting. It was like he was holding her there in the clouds just for her own pleasure, for a breath and another breath, and then she knew she was going to go over the edge of the cloud, and dive into his blue eyes as her body contracted with the peak of the tension. She groaned and tilted her head back, breathing hard, enjoying the energy ripping through her body as she gracefully floated back down to earth.

"I haven't finished with you yet," said Blaise.

"Oh," she heaved while looking at him and realized he was wearing way too many clothes. "It all comes off eventually." She winked as she reached forward and undid his jeans and tugged them down along with his jocks.

"That's better." He was erect and ready. She reached out to his cock and ran her fingers along the shaft. It contracted with her touch. Then she teased the tip of his cock until he groaned.

"Wait." He fully removed the last of his clothing and then fumbled around with his wallet.

She slipped her hand around to his cock and began to massage him slowly, enjoying the feel of the hardness in her hand and the moisture that eased from the tip. She helped him put the condom on and pulled him back on her, and rolled him over so she was on top.

"Oh, yes, you like to be on top," he said, his hands resting easily on her hips.

"Hell, yeah." She leaned forward kissing him, moving her breasts along his chest. She ached to have him inside. Her muscles wanted something to grip onto this time. She sat up and moved her hips, guiding him into her. She groaned as he slipped into her and her muscles enveloped around him.

She moved back and forth, slowly, her muscles gripping him with each forward thrust, and she felt herself rise with him this time. He moved his fingers back to her slit, and her body convulsed with pleasure as he found her spot once more. She increased her movements making them quicker as her breath shallowed, and his fingers moved in time with the rhythm she set. She could feel him inside her, hard and long, and she kept moving, urging them closer to their peak.

Tension built between them once more, harder and faster, the heat increased, and their breath quickened until they both toppled over the edge and were left heaving and gasping from the burst of pressure rippling through them.

Dusty rolled off of him, puffing hard from the exertion. She lay back in the wool. He turned over, and kissed her. She looked into his blue eyes. "That was worth waiting for." He tangled his legs and arms with her in a tight embrace as they returned from the bliss.

She rested her head on his chest. "It sure was."

CHAPTER 15

THE SHED WAS PITCH BLACK. Blaise didn't want to move. They'd spent the afternoon entwined with each other in the wool. Now, he just wanted to lie with Dusty in his arms with her head resting on his chest.

"Can you live out here?" Dusty lifted her head from his chest to look at him.

His mind froze. All he could think about was how much more he wanted to be around her, yet, there was a real world out beyond the shed. So far, country life hadn't agreed with him. *But maybe it could if I gave it a proper chance?*

Blaise remained silent. His thoughts tangled in his mind. He hadn't even been sure if anything was going to happen between them. This afternoon was a welcome surprise. When he had arrived, he was hoping for a dinner date with Dusty tonight. In the afterglow, his mind wasn't working. He was facing losing his job, and now Dusty was asking a tough question.

"Well, can you live here, on a farm, doing hard work for the rest of your life?" Her tone sharpened.

It was as if his brain melted in the heat, he couldn't think, couldn't speak. All he needed to say was yes. Yes, he could live here. Yes, he could do hard labor on the farm for the rest of his living life as long as it meant he could be with her. But his mouth didn't move. His throat didn't produce a sound. It was like he'd been possessed into silence.

"That's what I thought." Dusty got up from the wool and began dressing quickly.

"Dusty... no..."

This was his chance to change things, he reached out, pulled her back down and cuddled her since he couldn't manage to speak. Instead, she pushed away and pulled on her shirt. "Hope you enjoyed your romp in the wool, now get the fuck off my land."

Right then, he wanted her even more. The fire in her blood stirred his body as she stalked off.

"Wait." But she was out of sight, her boots clunking the metal ramp. "Dusty?" he yelled. He rushed to the door, naked, not caring about clothes. He heard an engine start, and by the time he looked out, her ute was gone.

"Damn." Blaise watched the lights of her ute disappear into the night as she drove down the paddock. *How do I keep managing to fuck things up with her?* He went back inside and dressed. He took his time hoping while she was gone, she'd cool down and come back in a state where they could talk. He could've gone into the house and waited, but with Claire around, he decided that would be too awkward. The silence was getting to him. All he could hear was the wind rattling the window of the shed. He couldn't bring himself to follow her, not after she stormed off like that.

There was only one option he could think of doing right now. Blaise got into his car and drove away, stunned. He didn't know where he was driving. He only knew that he'd blown up something that could've been so special. *Why couldn't I've just said yes?* Because country life hadn't been in his future plans. His plans were crumbling around him, and he thought very soon he too would start to turn to dust.

Dusty was a smart woman. She wouldn't want an excuse, or an apology, only the truth. *Not now. I can't say, sorry, but you weren't in my future plans, honey. See ya later.* He hit the steering wheel in frustration. *I could say, hey you fucked my brains out, and I couldn't think properly.* Blaise doubted she'd buy that one. To have gotten past her frozen walls for things to end up like this made Blaise angry.

All he could think of was going back to the city. The openness out here was causing him to lose himself. *If I could just get back to the city, soak up the noise, and the business. Breathe in some carbon dioxide then*

I could think more clearly. His blood ran cold at the thoughts.

Blaise was scared.

What if I'm happier in the city without her? The thought of losing her didn't sit right with him. But right now, he had to be honest, he wasn't sure if this was the life for him. He hated himself for that. He wasn't sure he could live out here, in the middle of nowhere, working hard every day. He wasn't sure that it was really the sort of life he wanted.

He wanted Dusty.

But she didn't come alone.

She came with a farm, responsibility, and hard work. Out here was a different world, and he'd fallen for one of the women, but now, now it was time to go home. He turned left at the intersection, and hoped this was the right road that would lead him back to Wilkton.

Was it just lust that attracted me to her? He had thought it was more. *Could've been more. I've made a right mess of this one.* This had felt different with Dusty. *Why can't things go smoothly?* It had for the time they had spent together. He sighed. Two more nights in this place, with countless cold showers, and he might survive the weekend. Now, all he wanted was to go back to Adelaide. He couldn't see anything happening with Dusty after what had happened.

This week had been so intense he'd almost forgotten what it was like in the city, he didn't even miss being away. Then there was another part of him who couldn't wait to get back to the lights and the noise of the cars, and to go to the pub with his mates and know he wasn't going to end up in a fight.

But he couldn't.

There was no way he was going to go back to Adelaide without talking to Dusty first. She was tired, confused, and scared under that hard, outer shell thanks to the bastard Aaron, and he knew he had to take things slow. He hit the steering wheel. *I should've gone slower.* He hit it again. *I shouldn't have slept with her.* He sighed. He didn't really regret that part. *I should've spoken up, told her about my job, more about my plans.* A twist in his gut made him realize that his plans didn't matter anymore. He was ready to throw them out and to make new ones. Especially if that meant he could be with her. He turned into the driveway of the Matilda's. He yawned. *She's tired. I'll speak to her tomorrow. I'll fix this.*

WHAT WAS I thinking letting a city boy into my life?

For once, she took time out for herself and had a good old romp in the wool. She couldn't believe they managed to hook up. *Was that only yesterday?* It must have been the easing of the sexual tension that had caused her mind to have a meltdown. There was too much bliss hanging around her head that she just blurted out the most stupid, inappropriate thing she could think of.

Can you live here?

What was I thinking?

Dusty rested her head on the tiled shower wall allowing the cool water to wash down her back. *God, he must think that if I have sex with someone, then we have to get married.* The question hadn't meant to be anything about commitment. She was just trying to gauge him a bit more, see if he wanted to live out here, not because she thought that they were now an item. But then she'd gone and kicked him out. *Good one, Dusty.* She'd just had great sex with a great looking guy. Their love-making had been tender, mind-blowing, and something she wanted more of. He'd opened up something in her, and she couldn't go back to the way things were. In the afterglow, it was like she'd had a flood of hormones or something, and her mouth took over and wanted a commitment from him, when that was the last thing she wanted or expected right now. They had to develop a relationship first, but no, she had to go and balls it up by asking him if he *can live here.*

Nothing like scaring off a man with a question like that. The problem was that she didn't want to scare him off. *I think I need a holiday. Relax for a bit.*

Dusty got out of the shower before she wasted too much rainwater. She dressed in clean clothes—jeans and a colorful short-sleeved shirt. It felt good to have the shearing done, and she'd spent the day working on the farm returning sheep to their paddocks and cleaning up after shearing. She kept herself busy. But Blaise still came into her mind a lot during the day. The image she had of him wasn't with him wearing a suit. She flushed with lustful heat. There had even been times during the day when she had looked around hoping to see his posh car. But he hadn't come.

I've got to see him. She'd put it off too long already.

Dusty knew if she really wanted to make something of a relationship with Blaise, then she should've been at his hotel room this morning. *What if he's gone back to Adelaide?* The thought twisted painfully in her stomach, and she quickly finished doing her hair.

Her mind kept getting caught on the details of their future. She couldn't move. And she didn't think he'd move, but oddly she didn't care so much about it. Not now. Not after getting to know him over the last few days. He really looked after her when she was upset in the pub, even though he was hurt himself. Dusty's heart pounded hard as she walked the hallway to the back door. He was a man worth pursuing, and she had to make things right.

"I'm heading out to town, should be back later tonight," said Dusty as she popped her head into the lounge room where her mom had her feet up watching television.

"I won't wait up," said Claire. "Enjoy yourself." She waved Dusty out.

Dusty hurried to her ute before she changed her

mind. She'd never chased after a guy before. Her heart felt lighter when she thought of Blaise, and she smiled.

The closer she got to the motel, the tighter her stomach became. She nearly lost her nerve and drove past the motel, but at the last minute, she drove in.

The last thing she wanted to do was to go and speak to Beryl, then everyone in town would know she was looking for Blaise and that would get some talking going. She drove past the rows of rooms that extended out to the left, looking for his Audi. Dusty couldn't see it. *Damn.* She didn't know what number room he was staying in.

He might be at the pub. She quickly turned her ute around and drove into town. *I have to patch things up with him.* The longer it took to find him, the more her stomach twisted. His car was nowhere in sight.

Lost at what to do next, Dusty drove to her friend's house. Bell would help her devise a plan on how to fix things up with Blaise.

Dusty couldn't help thinking Blaise was a new stud ram that was too good to turn away, but had now gone looking for greener pastures. *I treated him like shit.* She didn't think Blaise would forgive her now. Let's face it, I wouldn't forgive me.

Dusty parked and knocked on her friend's front door.

"Coming." She heard some banging deep within the house then the door opened. "Dusty."

"Wanna go out?"

"What happened?"

"Nothing." Dusty pushed past Bell into her home. She walked down the hallway to the back of the old Cornish-style house to the kitchen-living area. A wave of emotion built up inside of her that she didn't want to let it out. She took some deep breaths to try and push it back to wherever it had come from inside of her.

"Ever since first grade, I've known when you were lying to me, so out with it." Bell closed the front door and followed her down the hallway.

Dusty flopped down on the lounge. "That smells nice. Watch ya cooking?" The smell of spaghetti bolognese took her mind off of her emotions. It was like having sex with Blaise unleashed forgotten hormones or something. One minute she felt great, then the next she was down because she hadn't managed to talk to him. She didn't know if she could take much more of this, but the good thing was she could start putting this all behind her, and she just knew a night out with Bell would help with that.

"Don't try and change the subject." Bell sat opposite and glared at her friend. "Tell me."

"Nothing. I'm starved. Got enough food for two?"

"You slept with him, didn't you?" gasped Bell. "Good for you."

"How did you know?" Dusty narrowed her eyes at her friend.

"I didn't, it was just a stab in the dark, but I know now." Bell smiled.

"Yeah, well, I ballsed it up now, didn't I?" Dusty leaned her head into the side of the lounge, wishing hard that things had unfolded differently between her and Blaise.

"Yep, that sounds like you."

"Thanks for your support." Dusty grabbed a cushion and hugged it in front of her.

"He didn't hurt you or anything?" asked Bell her facing creasing with seriousness.

"No, of course not. It was all me and my big mouth."

Bell let out a deep sigh. "Go and talk to him."

"I'm not sure where he is."

"Oh." Bell thought for a moment. "We can try the pubs."

"Already did but couldn't see his car."

"Did you go inside?"

Dusty shook her head and slumped back in the lounge. "Yeah, I was a bit slow on this one."

She'd been so busy pushing forward with farm work, pushing Aaron away, that she hadn't realized her heart had begun to turn for Blaise. *A city boy of all people.* But that was one city boy she was going to have to put out of her mind.

"You might see him again."

"Maybe." But Dusty really felt like she'd blown it. They were worlds apart, and it was better to let him go.

It wasn't the easiest thing to do after they'd just had sex, and she couldn't get him out of her mind or the idea of getting back in his pants again.

"I'll forget him in time."

"This sounds like self-protection mode to me."

"What?" Bell liked to read pop psych books and was always rattling off some theory about relationships, the universe, and manifesting your reality.

"You're not going to pursue him because this could be the real thing, and you don't want the pain of getting hurt."

"You're making my brain hurt." She rubbed her forehead as if to make her point.

"No, I'm not. You are."

"What?" She threw the cushion at Bell, who caught it and threw it back. It missed and landed short on the floor.

"I'm sure you had a good time together when you... well... you know," said Bell.

Dusty's cheeks turned deep red.

"Don't give up so easily."

"I'm not. I'm being realistic." Dusty didn't have it in her to chase Blaise.

She'd lost her nerve. And not after she'd made a fool of herself. *He wouldn't want me now.*

"You're not." Bell glared at her. "I don't want you missing out on a good thing."

Dusty knew Blaise was more than a good thing.

She took a deep breath and froze. "Hey, is something burning?"

"Shit." Bell jumped up and ran over to the stove. "Oh, no." She took the lid off the saucepan. A mixture of steam and smoke flooded out. "Quick, open the door before the smoke alarm goes off."

Dusty jumped up and opened the sliding door in the back while Bell opened the kitchen windows. "Fancy take out?"

"Or, we could just go to the pub? I'm starved."

Bell put the saucepan in the sink. "The pub it is."

Dusty rested back on the bench and yawned. "All of this is making me feel tired. I think I need a holiday."

"You sure do."

"But I can't afford much. Is going to Adelaide for a week considered a holiday?"

"No, but if that's all you've got available, then it's better than nothing."

"Wanna come with me?"

"Sorry, you know I'd love to live it up in the city for a week, but I'm saving my holidays for a trip overseas next year."

"I know."

"Go, stay with your sister. That will save you paying for accommodation."

Dusty had some money set aside but she wanted to keep it. She had to. Things weren't so easy on the farm, and she needed some money in the bank for when machinery broke, or for vet bills, or for fertilizer or spraying equipment. Holidays were a luxury. "I'll ring Jody later."

"Good. And I'll check up on you to make sure you do. Holidays are very good at clearing the mind, and you're in need of that."

"Thanks a lot."

"Just saying it as it is." She winked at Dusty.

"I plan to keep my legs crossed." Dusty smiled.

Bell always had a way of cheering her up. "But I think I'll stick with a simple holiday and nothing more for now. I'm too worn out."

"Boring. I bet you wouldn't keep them crossed if a certain boy met you. One called Blaise." She left the room before Dusty could answer. "I'll change, then we can go."

Dusty blushed glad Bell wasn't able to see her. Blaise just didn't have the sticking power to tough it out here in the country. *If he did, he wouldn't have run back to the city.* She just had to accept, no matter how she felt, that Blaise was a dust cloud that had blown away.

CHAPTER 16

"Two pints," said Dusty to the waitress behind the bar. She leaned hard on the bar to keep herself upright. *I'm celebrating now that shearing is done.* But that wasn't the real reason for her drinking. She kept telling herself this every time she thought of Blaise. *Forget him.*

Dusty took the two drinks back to the table where Bell and she were sitting.

"This is the last drink," said Bell. They'd done a round of shots before and were now back drinking beer. "I'm fast reaching my limit."

"That can't be true. Your limit's high." Dusty raised her glass. "To having a holiday."

"To holidays." Bell clinched her glass with Dusty's. "And make sure you do take one."

"Yes, ma'am." Dusty gave a fake salute then took a gulp of her beer. She pulled a face. "Why did I get beer?"

"It's cheap. And you do like it." Bell giggled.

"I do, but this isn't tasting right."

"That's because you're mixing your drinks." Aaron dragged over a chair and sat at the table with them.

Dusty looked up and narrowed her eyes. "You weren't invited." She hadn't seen Aaron come in, but after the number of drinks she'd consumed, she was no longer looking over her shoulder to see who came into the pub.

Earlier in the night when she did look, she secretly hoped against all the odds Blaise would come in. But no. He'd up and left her because she was stupid and couldn't hold her tongue or her temper sending him a clear message she didn't want him. And now she had to talk to Aaron.

"I'm sure you ladies won't mind," said Aaron.

"Well, we do, so bugger off," said Bell. She gave him a stern look.

"I just want to join in the fun."

"Been in any fights lately?" asked Dusty.

"I told the city boy who's boss."

Bell smirked. "Not the way I hear it."

Dusty tried not to laugh. "Is that right?" She leaned forward to look at his face. "Looks like he taught you a lesson."

"Ya should've seen him."

"I did," said Dusty.

Aaron's face clouded over. "Could ya give us a minute, Bell?"

"No," said Bell and Dusty together.

"I've told you I don't want you," said Dusty.

"But you didn't mean it." He put on a demure face.

"Don't fall for it," said Bell.

"I won't." Dusty stood up. "I'm going to the ladies."

She had to get out of there, get away from Aaron. She was so angry at Aaron for hitting her and for him hitting Blaise too. She had loved him for a bit, before his anger got in the way, not now. But with her head overrun and unable to process things properly because of the alcohol and because of Blaise, she needed to get away from Aaron before she did something she regretted.

God, I'm out of control.

She pushed the bathroom door open with force, and it slammed shut behind her. Dusty splashed cold water on her face and patted it dry with some paper towels. *Aaron wouldn't be a bad option.* She threw the paper in the bin, took a deep breath. *No. He'd be a terrible option.* With a long, deep breath she tried to compose herself.

Time to go home. She walked down the gray-lit hallway, back toward the front bar. Someone grabbed her arm and pulled her back.

"Hey," she yelled.

Dusty looked up into Aaron's eyes. She saw the old flame there, fading, but it was there.

"Let me go." Her voice didn't have the resolve in it like before. He had a way of getting to her when she was least expecting it. Old emotions fired inside of her.

"Aaron…"

"I'm sorry, Dusty… for the other day…." he paused, "… I've been lost without you. I want you." His eyes were watery.

"But Aaron—"

"Dusty, I'm sorry. I'm sorry. I'm sorry." His voice softened with each sorry, the words vibrated around her in a soothing embrace.

He leaned forward and kissed her. She felt herself weaken in his embrace. It was different to Blaise. When Aaron kissed her, an electric shot of lightning coursed through her body, and then another one as he brushed his tongue against hers, hard and tough. It was what she was used to. All her thoughts moved around in her head, scrambled out of place as she let him kiss her, and worse, she kissed him back.

BLAISE SANG to the music on the radio during the half hour trip back to Wilkton. He'd spent the day looking around the local area, checking out the attractions, and seeing a few people who asked him to look over their books. Word seemed to have gotten out that he was a reliable accountant and saved people money. He was picking up new clients much faster than he thought possible.

What he really would have liked to do was spent the day with Dusty. He would've liked her to show him around. But no matter how much he wanted to go to her, he didn't. He needed to clear his thoughts first. That's what he'd been doing at the beach. It just took much longer than he had anticipated. Now it was dark and too late to see Dusty.

I'll see her tomorrow.

His heart pounded quicker as he thought of her. While he'd been thinking of Dusty a lot today, he still hadn't gotten enough of her. His emotions were settled, and he knew that he wanted Dusty. He was going to go and get his own little dusty cloud. He was sure he could talk his way out of why he didn't answer her earlier.

He drove through Wilkton and saw Dusty's ute at Ol' Billies. Without a second thought, he parked his car and went inside. He pushed the front door of the pub open and walked in. It wasn't busy. He looked around for Dusty.

"You must be Blaise," said a girl about Dusty's age.

"And you are?" Blaise looked over her head trying to find Dusty.

"Bell. Dusty's best friend."

"Do you know where she is?" He looked at Bell intensely. "I have to find her. It's important."

Bell's face dropped and looked over to the door in the corner. Blaise took the hint and went there. He couldn't wait any longer. He had to speak with her and sort out this mess.

Blaise bumped his way between people and pushed through the door. It took a moment for his eyes to adjust, and then a moment to process what he was seeing.

He stood frozen.

Dusty was there in the shadows.

His gut twisted.

She was kissing another man.

Worse.

It was Aaron.

Blaise spun around and left. He'd seen enough. *Last straw.* What could've been between them was no longer a possibility.

He bumped into someone.

"Hey, Blaise, what's going on?" asked Bell.

Blaise brushed past her and stalked to the front door.

Blaise didn't hear anymore as he weaved his way out of the pub, the heat of so many people in a confined space burned his skin. The cool night air slapped him as he stepped outside. He kicked a can into the gutter and it rattled empty across the concrete ground.

Only a country boy would suit her.

"Blaise, wait," yelled Bell. "Blaise."

He kept walking down the street. *What a wasted trip.* The thought was bitter in his mind.

Bell ran up to him. "Blaise, stop for a sec." She grabbed his arm and forced him to turn around.

"What on earth can you say to make this situation any better?" he asked her.

Bell puffed. "She's drunk."

"Not helping."

"She's confused."

"And I'm meant to buy that?"

"I'm hoping so because I think you two would be great together."

"You don't know me?" He shook his arm free from her grip.

"Call it a woman's intuition."

"So, I'm meant to forgive her?"

"Well, that would be a start. You know Aaron is rough."

"She's kissing him." He turned and walked down the street.

Bell ran to catch up and struggled to keep up with his fast stride. "We all make mistakes."

"And I'm done making them with her."

"Just, just... don't give up on her. Please."

"She's made her choice."

He got in, slammed the door shut forcing Bell to jump out of the way, and drove off spinning his wheels and marking the road with rubber.

~

Dusty tried to push Aaron away but he held her tight, pinching her waist and continuing the kiss she'd stopped returning. She hadn't been thinking of Aaron. It was Blaise who she thought of when kissing Aaron. Suddenly, the bolt of lust that Aaron sent flying through her body disappeared. Her thoughts, as clouded as they were from drinking too much, ordered in her brain.

She pushed her hands on his chest, hard and firm, and turned her head. "No."

"Come on, you're giving me mixed messages."

"My message was clear when I kicked you the other night," she answered. She felt his body tense in anger. *I'm ready for him.*

He let her go. "You bitch."

"You've called me that before, and look at you, back here for more." She slid her back along the wall to get further away from him. "What? You can't find anyone else?"

Aaron raised his hand but then paused as someone came through the door. He stepped back to let them pass. Dusty used the chance to walk away.

"Come back," said Aaron.

"Go to hell," answered Dusty. She turned to glare at him. "Come near me again, and it's your balls I'll kick." She pushed through the door into the main pub area looking around for Bell.

"You're a fuckin' tease," said Aaron quietly behind her. "You need a man to put you right."

"I said, *no.*" Dusty glared at Aaron. People in the pub went quiet. "You want a scene to prove how much I hate you?"

Aaron narrowed his eyes. "What could you do to prove that..." He didn't finish. Dusty snapped and kicked her boot into his groin. Hard. Aaron doubled over groaning in pain.

"Do you get it now or should I kick you again?" Dusty clenched her fists ready.

Aaron glared at her, but Dusty saw a change in his eyes. She felt satisfaction ripple through her. Someone pulled her back.

"What the hell have you done?" she demanded to Dusty.

Dusty swallowed hard. "Gave him what he deserves."

"I'm not talking about Aaron, stupid. Blaise just stormed off."

"Blaise was here?" Dusty couldn't believe it. *He was here. Shit. He must have seen me kissing Aaron.* Oh. My. God. Bile rose up into Dusty's mouth.

The room swayed and mucous rose up Dusty's throat. *Oh no.* She cupped her hand over her mouth and dashed to the bathroom. Dusty's night of drinking spilled out into the toilet along with her hopes of talking to Blaise, of starting a relationship.

"Are you okay?" asked Bell gently as she came into the cubicle. She rubbed her hand on Dusty's back.

"I've made a mess of things," said Dusty. She retched into the bowl again.

"I'm going to have to agree with you there," said Bell softly. "What were you thinking?"

Dusty shook her head. "He caught me off guard. Wouldn't…"

When her mind did kick into gear, it was Blaise she wanted to be kissing. Her stomach twisted as she thought of Blaise seeing her kiss Aaron. *And to think I'd come into town just to see him.* Heat welled behind her eyes.

"Come on, let's get you home," said Bell helping Dusty to stand.

"Was he… was… he…?" Dusty couldn't bring herself to ask about Blaise's reaction.

"Angry. Pissed off. Confused." Bell guided her out of the bathroom.

Not a good way to start a relationship, thought Dusty bitterly. *More like the perfect way to end one.*

Dusty held her breath against the sensation of nausea as she walked gingerly to the car. "What a day."

"Yes, you won't be forgetting this in a hurry."

No, I won't, thought Dusty as she rested her head against the coolness of the car window. She desperately wished she could forget. She pushed the thoughts from her mind about how differently the night could've ended if she hadn't kissed Aaron.

That was what hurt her the most.

The thoughts of what could've been.

CHAPTER 17

Blaise dumped his box of office belongings on his kitchen table. He went straight to the fridge and took out a beer. He'd been fired. He was almost expecting that, but he'd surprised himself when he argued with his boss to try and keep his job. *What was I thinking?* The argument got heated, so heated they were both yelling at each other, and in the end, Danny threatened to call security.

Blaise swallowed a gulp of beer. *If only I had walked out then and not told him I wouldn't want to work for his pathetic business.* There'd been more, but Blaise drank some more beer to forget about what he said. He'd crossed a few lines in a matter of seconds, and he'd well and truly burned his bridges there. *No going back now.*

With the help of the beer, the build-up of adrenaline in his body began to dissipate. Blaise took a deep breath. He was definitely on his own now. But he wasn't feeling elated about the prospect. *Probably 'cause I know how much hard work it's going to be.* He'd been working for Danny since he'd finished university. It was the longest place he'd worked at, and he now had to readjust his plans big time for his future. Not exactly what he'd planned to be doing at twenty-eight.

His phone rang. He checked the number to make sure it wasn't anyone from the office he was no longer part of. He didn't recognize the phone number. "Hello?"

"Hi, Blaise, did I get you at a bad time?"

"No, Claire." He missed seeing Dusty too, which didn't help how he was feeling at the moment. He wanted to see her again, more so now since he knew that she wasn't with Aaron.

"Just wondering how you're getting on with the accounts?"

"Good, there's a bit of savings I've found. I'll send you the documents to sign if you like."

He was surprised Claire was ringing since he'd already told her this information.

"Great. Um... you know Aaron's no longer in the picture? Dusty's given him the boot once and for all."

So that's the real reason she's calling. He was already up with this part of the gossip.

"Good for her."

The reminder stirred the feelings toward Dusty that he was trying to suppress.

"Oh, and when you send the forms, can you make sure you send them to me? Dusty's really precious about doing this work herself, and I want her to see the savings first. Once she does, she'll be more likely to agree to have you do the accounts."

"Sure. I'll probably need some more documents, too. I'll make a list and then let you know."

"Good, talk soon then. Bye."

"Bye."

Blaise saved the number in his contacts. If he rang this number, he wouldn't have to speak to Dusty, and right now that suited him just fine.

He picked up his half-drunk beer and went into his office. "Now is as good as time as any." He began entering data. He might be out of a job, but now he had his own business to start. He had a lot of work ahead of him, which was the perfect way to try and forget about a certain girl.

CHAPTER 18

Dusty had put off the promise to herself to go on holiday for three months. There was always an excuse. She had to take the bales of wool to Adelaide. The weather turned early and then on the tractor planting this year's crops. All valid reasons not to go away from the farm. Now, it was well into June, and she was keeping an eye on the ewes giving birth to lambs. She wasn't about to go anywhere, holiday or not. She needed to be here running the farm. More importantly, she wanted to be on the farm doing this work.

Dusty came inside from the cold, kicked her muddy boots off by the back door, walked into the bathroom, and washed up for dinner.

"Sure, I've written down the details and will meet you Friday," said her mom into her phone.

Dusty immediately became curious. She yawned

and stretched out her back before walking into the kitchen. "Who was that?"

"The new accountant I was telling you about," said her mom. She put down the phone. "Ready for dinner?"

"Sure, so who's this new accountant, and can we afford him?" Dusty didn't like her mom going ahead and organizing things on the farm without running it by her first. When she realized the books were missing, she'd been furious with her mom for giving them to an accountant without asking her. She wanted to do them herself, which was rather ambitious, but it would save them money. As usual, the farm jobs got in the way, and she let it slide.

"Just some city boy who came highly recommended." Claire turned on the frying pan. "You okay with chops and mashed tonight?"

"Sure." She got up and took out two potatoes and began peeling them. A simple staple meal for tonight would more than satisfy her after driving around checking sheep all day.

"Lambing going okay?" asked her mom.

"Yeah, no trouble today." She cut up the potato into squares and threw them into the hot water. They had lost at least two lambs to foxes. She'd kept a close eye out for any foxes but hadn't managed to catch them.

"They're just about finished lambing." Dusty put the lid on the pot.

"Good. Then maybe you could go to town on Friday and see the accountant."

"Why not you?"

"You promised to take a break from the farm," said her mom as she put the chops in the frying pan.

"Yeah, but you know how hard it is to leave a farm."

"Which is why I'm trying to get you to go to town on Friday. Stay with your sister for the weekend and then come back Monday. I can keep an eye on things here."

"I don't know."

"Well, if you don't trust me, you could ask James to help. He'll be all right checking the ewes to make sure none of them are having trouble lambing."

The idea of taking a few days off farm work would be great, but then she hated going to the city. The noise drove her mad, and the pollution clogged her lungs. To her, the city stunk worse than a dead sheep. Give her fresh air any day even if it was tainted with the smell of sheep poo.

"It would be good for you to see Jody, check in on her, and make sure she's doing okay."

"I'm sure she's doing just fine."

"Yeah, but you could check in on her."

Dusty knew this was her mom's way of making sure she got away from the farm for a few days. Her sister kept in regular contact and was doing just fine, so she didn't really need to check up on her. She'd even started a relationship with a guy.

Who I haven't met yet. Maybe that would be a better reason to go to town, check out this person who her little sister's dating. "Fine then, I'll take the accounts, and if Jody doesn't mind, I'll stay with her for a few days."

"She doesn't mind, she's expecting you at her place Friday afternoon."

"You were expecting me to say yes all along?"

"No... I was just hoping you would, Dusty. You need to get away from the farm sometimes, you know."

"I know, but I do love it here." Nothing got her excited like sitting on the tractor going around in circles for hours day after day. That was her thinking and planning time. She got to listen to music and podcasts and catch up on what was going on locally and around the world.

"Too much sometimes."

"I don't know how I'm going to survive in her small apartment, but at least I'll get to see this new guy of hers before you." She could play this game too. "Unless you want to go down instead of me?"

"I know what you're doing, and it's not going to work." Her mom gave her a dark look. "I expect a full report of this young man Jody's dating when you get back, and if you decide to stay longer, that's fine with me. I'll keep an eye on things."

"No way. I've got too much to do here." Dusty checked the potatoes and turned down the heat to stop them from boiling over. "You've been dealing with this accountant, so on second thoughts, you should go."

Her mom sighed. "You do need a break sometime."

"I know, just not now."

The problem was that by Thursday, things changed. Her mom had the flu, and there was no way she was able to drive down to the city.

"Fine, I'll go," said Dusty. "Only because if we don't get the tax done soon, we face getting a fine."

"Thanks," said Claire the word pinched because of her blocked nose. "Stay there over the weekend, too. I'll be fine without you." She blew her nose.

"I don't know."

"I'll get Val to drop in on me."

"Okay, I'll go ring James and see if he can keep an eye on the sheep for you and make sure they have enough feed."

The problem in winter, after the rains, was that there was often too much green grass, and she had to feed out hay to give the sheep some variety in what they ate. It was a good position in some ways since it meant there was plenty of rain, but in others, it meant more work and another cost if she had to buy in hay.

FRIDAY MORNING, Dusty was up early to go through the jobs that James had to do over the next few days. There wasn't much to be done, and Dusty had to admit that this was really the best time to go to Adelaide. Her phone beeped, a message from Jody.

> Can't wait to see you sis. Stay in town
> Fri after meeting and we can go
> shopping

"Just what I don't need to be doing," said Dusty when she read the text from her sister. She didn't need any new clothes, at least not the sort of clothes her sister would be looking at.

> Sounds good, c u later tonight Arcade café.

The Arcade café was the only place Dusty knew where to go for good coffee in the city, and she was also meeting the accountant there first. It made things easier for her as all she had to do was sit there and wait for her sister instead of going somewhere else in the city.

> OK. Will text you when in city. Meet
> you there at 4

Dusty drove to Adelaide in her ute. She'd even found time to clean it quickly to get rid of some of the mud on the outside. With the music up loud, the two-hour trip didn't feel so long. *This accountant better be worth paying.*

The closer to Adelaide she drove, the more her nerves fluttered in her stomach. *And he better be worth this trouble.*

She noticed the traffic as soon as she drove into

town. Cars were behind her, in front of her, and on each side of her along the three-lane highway. It made her jumpy. During peak time at home in Wilkton she could drive down the main road, and the only cars near her were parked. If there was someone behind her, they were well behind, and she barely registered they were there. But here, in the city, the cars were so close she'd begun to break out in a cold sweat.

Dusty memorized the route to take to get her into the city, to the car park on Rundle Street, the only one she was vaguely familiar with.

She always checked her blind spot before changing lanes but was still honked at a few times, enough so when she turned into the car park, she was shaking. It didn't help having to drive a big ute around in such a confined space. She could drive tractors, trucks, and other heavy machinery, but she had space for it at the farm. Here, in the city, it seemed there wasn't any room for a ute.

Gripping the steering wheel tightly, Dusty slowly drove up the levels searching for a free space. There was one, but she thought it was too small and so she kept going becoming more anxious she wouldn't find a park.

At the sixth level, there were plenty, and she parked well away from other cars, more for her own piece of mind. And even though she could reverse a truck and trailer, parking so close to other vehicles like this further frayed her nerves. Dusty walked to the lift repeating six, six, six in her mind, so she wouldn't forget what level she was on.

When Dusty got to the ground level, she decided she couldn't remember if she'd locked the ute or not, and since her overnight bag was still in the ute, she went back up to the sixth level to check. A good thing because out of habit, she hadn't locked the ute.

Back down at the ground level, she walked Rundle Mall to the Arcade café her mom told her to go to meet the accountant. She realized now she had no idea what his name was.

Dusty checked the time on her phone. She was about fifteen minutes late which wasn't bad in some ways considering she'd just driven one hundred and fifty K's to get to the city.

She walked into the café and looked around for someone who she thought might look like an accountant. Most tables had more than one person sitting at them, and she figured she was looking for someone sitting alone. She went further into the café. A man sat alone around the corner, and she started heading toward him.

Dusty froze.

Blaise sat there with a pile of papers in front of him, twirling a silver pen between his fingers.

Her jaw dropped.

He looked even sexier than she remembered.

Dusty ran her hands down the side of her jeans and took a deep breath. She was already flushed from the sight of him. He suddenly looked up. They stared at each other, both uncertain what to say or do.

Guess it's best to get this over with. Dusty stepped toward him. *He's only a guy*, she tried to remind herself, *a guy she had sex with*. One that was causing her pulse to increase and butterflies to swim in her stomach.

You're over him. She lied to herself and forced herself to walk up to him as if this was no big deal.

He smiled.

Her heart pounded stronger and caused her chest to ache. She never thought it was possible for someone to have such an effect on her.

"Good to see you again." She held out her hand.

Best keep this meeting as professional as possible.

Blaise hesitated before taking her hand. The touch of his soft hand sent shivers up her arm right to her heart and down to fuel the heat between her thighs. His handshake was firm and strong. She remembered another part of his body firm and strong. Heat flushed over her cheeks.

"I wasn't expecting you," he said as she sat down.

"Didn't Mom tell you she couldn't come?" She placed her handbag on her lap, unsure what to do with her worldly wealth with so many people around. Back home she'd carelessly put the bag on the floor near her or on the back of the chair, but she was in the city now and had to be more careful. Her mouth dried like a summer with no rain.

Blaise shook his head.

"Sorry, but you'll have to do with me."

"You'll do fine." He cleared his throat and shuffled the papers.

She saw his fingers tremble slightly. "I hope you don't charge too much?"

"I'm guessing your mom hasn't told you much then?"

"No."

"Ah, well then, um… I'm not charging to do this. It's just a once-off to help you guys out since you were so kind during my stay in the country."

That wasn't how Dusty remembered treating him, and it wasn't how Bell told her she'd treated Blaise.

"You're doing this for free?"

"Yes. I thought I could find some savings to help you out."

"And did you?" She stared into his blue eyes in shock. *I've really misjudged him.*

"Yes. Here." He handed over a spreadsheet of figures. "I'll get you a coffee. Cappuccino?" He stood up.

"I don't want to put you out."

"You're not. Cappuccino?"

Dusty looked at Blaise over the top of the paper, and her breath caught in her throat. Heat concentrated low in her abdomen as she soaked in his appearance. His black hair was neat, a long cut, his eyes blue and clear, and he looked smart in the suit pants and shirt. *No*, she corrected. *He looks sexy and downright fuckable.*

Dusty nodded. She watched him walking away in confident strides as he went over to the counter to order for her. He looked even better than she'd imagined over the last few months. She looked at the numbers on the sheet, to stop herself from staring at his tight butt as he waited to order.

It was hard for Dusty to absorb the figures and what they meant. Blaise had done a great job presenting the information and how much they were going to save.

Blaise returned with her coffee and another one for himself. "So, what do you think?"

She smelled his spicy aftershave as he sat the cup next to her. Her head spun pleasantly from his scent. "Wow."

"Phew." Blaise's face relaxed. "I was worried there for a bit that you weren't going to be satisfied."

If only you knew.

"The savings will help a lot. Thank you." She put the paper down. "I should pay you for your services."

"No. It wasn't the agreement."

"I'm not sure—"

"Please accept it. Take it as a once-off if you like."

Dusty sat back. Whenever she'd accepted help from Aaron, she felt guilty after. But here with Blaise, that wasn't the case. She was grateful he'd take the time to help out and not expect anything in return. His sincerity embraced her like a warm hug.

"Okay then. On one condition..." She was feeling

confident, daring, willing to try something. It was the heat in her thighs, the sight of him fueling her desire for him, and her confidence rose.

"What?"

"You let me take you out to dinner."

She may have made a mess of things before. Now she could change that, one step at a time. The first being dinner and for now only dinner. She wanted more. To rip off his shirt and take in his toned chest, run her fingers over his hot skin, but no. One step at a time.

Blaise looked shocked. "I'm not used to a woman paying."

"Consider it a once-off."

He laughed. "Fine then. Tomorrow night. But I get to choose where we go."

"Don't make it too expensive." Dusty clamped her mouth shut. That wasn't what she meant to say. She was so used to keeping track of her money and not spending unnecessarily.

"It won't be. But then I'll have to add another condition to the evening."

"Okay," Dusty hesitated.

"I'll pick you up and drive."

"Don't you want to come along in the ute?"

"I'd love to, but this is my home area, and we get to do things my way."

"Except, I pay for dinner."

"That will be the only exception."

"I'm not sure what I've gotten myself into."

"A night of fun with me, I should hope."

His comment made her feel at ease. "So, would you like me to finalize your tax form, which is now overdue, but if you give me the go ahead, I could get it in just in time to possibly avoid a fine."

"Really? You'll get them to wave the fine?"

"Can't guarantee, but I can give it a go."

"Thanks." Every little savings helped. She wished they weren't so hard-up financially.

"Pleasure."

Maybe Blaise was a blessing after all. She looked at the figures and how much he was saving, it was thousands. "How did you manage such a savings?"

"There were a few new government tax breaks that weren't being claimed."

Since Dusty did the forms herself, she wouldn't have known about these tax breaks.

"I have them here for you to sign." He took out some more forms from his satchel.

"I think we're going to have to employ you for the future, I hope your rates aren't too high."

"I can do something special for you." He handed her a pen. "Just sign here."

She smiled. "I feel like I'm signing more than just a tax form."

"Just the form." He winked at her.

Dusty's heart fluttered, and the pen wobbled a little as she signed the papers. It was good to finally be on top of the tax. She'd let it slip way too much because she was worried about how much she'd end up paying. If he offered affordable rates, then that would help out and take away a job that she didn't really have the skills or the inclination to do. "About the other time... I didn't... well... I didn't mean what happened." Her cheeks turned red.

"It's forgotten. In the past now."

"But... I just wanted you to know—"

"Clean slate, then?"

"Sounds good." She sighed with relief.

"Dusty."

She jumped at the sound of her name. She turned and saw her sister all dressed up in her city attire, a funky bright dress with colored wool sewn in swirls on a black tailored dress and a multicolor scarf that was so long it almost reached her knees. Dusty stood up, and they hugged.

"We're just finishing here," she said to Jody. "This is our new accountant, Blaise."

"Pleased to meet you." Jody shook hands with Blaise.

"I feel part of the family now that I've met everyone."

"Thanks for all of your help, Blaise, I'll see you later."

"Wait."

Dusty stopped. She'd suddenly gotten all shy and was about to hurry away.

"I need an address to pick you up."

"Oh, um… of course."

She took the pen he held out for her and wrote down her sister's address on the back of his business card.

"I'll see you at seven sharp tomorrow evening," said Blaise.

"She'll be there," stated Jody.

"Bye." Dusty walked away forcing her sister to run to catch up.

"So, what's with you and Blaise?" asked Jody.

"Nothing."

They walked down the mall. The number of people milling around was giving Dusty a headache, and the noise was beginning to get to her. *So much chatter.* It smelled like a wet dog. *Ted doesn't even smell this bad.*

"Aren't you two going out to dinner tomorrow night?"

"And that's all."

"Yeah, right. I saw how you two were looking at each other."

"Just dinner since he did the tax for free."

"You're blushing." Jody grabbed hold of Dusty's hand. "Right, you need a proper outfit. You need to wear a dress."

"No, I don't."

"You do, and I'm willing to have a hissy fit in public to make sure you have something sexy to wear."

"Jody, you're too old for that."

"Yep." She raised her voice. "He's worth—"

Dusty clamped her hand over Jody's mouth and only just managed to muffle whatever it was she was going to say. "Okay."

She'd go shopping, but she was sure they wouldn't find anything that would be suitable, or anything that she'd like or be comfortable wearing.

Jody wrestled out of her sister's grip. "Do you even know when you last wore a dress?"

Dusty paused, thinking. Heat rose to her cheeks as she remembered the picnic with Blaise.

"Come on, I know exactly where we should look first."

Before Dusty could protest any more, Jody grabbed her hand and dragged her into a rather expensive shop.

Dusty groaned.

This was going to be a long evening.

CHAPTER 19

"My head is about to explode," said Dusty. She rubbed her temples as she stood in the center of the dressing rooms while Jody checked over the dress she tried on.

"It suits you," said the shop assistant.

"No, it's not for me," said Dusty.

The constant noise of city life, traffic, people talking, music, buskers seemed to reverberate in her head. She couldn't think anymore. So far, she refused to buy any dresses, but Jody was fast wearing her down.

"I think we'll try the other dress," said Jody.

"What, you agree with me?" asked Dusty.

"Maybe, but I want to see the other dress first." Jody pushed Dusty back into the dressing room as the shop assistant went off to rehang the dresses that weren't wanted.

"I think we should go home. I can't try on any more dresses."

"Do you want to look your best tomorrow night?"

Dusty sighed as she pulled the curtains closed in the dressing room. She wanted to wear something she was comfortable in. She didn't think wearing her jeans and dress boots were going to be suitable for dinner, unless they went to a fast-food place, and she didn't want to be going there. "My boots are clean."

"Yeah, but there's this faint smell of sheep poo on them."

Dusty groaned as she slipped out of the dress. She took the other dress off the hanger and put it on. The material slipped through her hands, soft and delicate. It was so different from what she was used to wearing. Even the city smelled different, like urine, waste, and car exhaust. She didn't think her boots smelled any worse than the city did.

"Are you done?"

"Nearly." Dusty looked in the mirror to make sure the dress was sitting right. It was made of a Lycra material, lined and emphasized her figure. Her bust had become twice the size. She looked at the price tag and nearly choked. She couldn't afford this even with Blaise saving them money. It was still too expensive. And it didn't quite cover her knees. "It's too short."

"Come out and let me see," said Jody. "Or I'll come in if you like."

"Don't you dare!" Dusty fussed with the dress for a

little longer, then decided to get this over with. She pushed open the curtains and stepped out. "This is the last dress I'm trying on."

"You better buy it then," said Jody.

"Can't afford it."

"You look great. It's not too flashy. It's a simple cut. Love the color of turquoise on you. It's perfect," said Jody.

She made Dusty turn around in front of the large mirror between the dressing rooms. "See, you look great."

"I feel like a stuffed chook." Dusty tried to pull the material away from her. "It's way too tight."

"Stop complaining, the jeans you wear are way too tight. Half the men in the mall are staring at your ass."

Dusty's eyes widened in horror. "They are not."

"Are to." Jody gave her another once over. "This is fine."

For a younger sister, Jody was certainly the bossy one.

"Wow," said the shop assistant. "That color is great on you."

"Come on, you want to be looking your best, even if nothing happens between you and Blaise."

Dusty forced herself to take another look in the mirror. She certainly didn't recognize the person standing there with a dress on. The dress was low cut, too low for what she was used to, so she tried to pull up the front of the dress.

"Oh no, that cleavage is perfect. Blaise won't keep his eyes off of you," said Jody.

"That's what I'm worried about," said Dusty.

"Well, don't be."

The dress had three-quarter sleeves and was snug around the waist then expanded out into a full skirt that ended just above her knees.

"I'll be too cold," said Dusty.

"I've got a black jacket you can borrow."

Dusty took another look. The shops were closing in about fifteen minutes, and her sister sounded tired. She had nearly won this round of not buying a dress. But when she looked at her reflection, she couldn't believe the dress actually looked all right on her. *Maybe this will be okay?*

"If anything, you'll make Blaise insanely jealous," said Jody.

"I don't think I want to be doing that," said Dusty.

"Sure, you do. He's a hot guy, smart, and there's certainly chemistry between you two."

"Is not."

"Is to. I could see it a mile away."

"Anyway, do this for yourself then. When was the last time you bought a piece of clothing for yourself?"

"End of last year before the start of harvest," answered Dusty proudly.

"Yeah, what?" Jody put her hands on her hips, challenging her sister to tell the truth. She had the same look on her face that her mom did when Dusty was trying to get out of something.

"I splashed out... RM Williams was having a sale. I got three new shirts and two new pairs of jeans."

"Work clothes, weren't they?"

Dusty felt a heat of anger rising up inside of her. "Yes, and there's nothing wrong with that."

"No, but you're not going to work tomorrow night." Jody got out her purse from her handbag. "I'll pay for half."

"You can't afford it."

"No, but I'm willing to take a chance. Besides, consider it part of your birthday gift."

"The one you haven't bought me for how many years?"

Jody wagged her finger at Dusty. "Yes. So, you better take it 'cause you might not get any more if you don't," she said in a mock telling-off tone.

Dusty laughed.

"We're closing up in five," said the shop assistant as she walked into the change rooms.

Dusty glanced in the mirror and made up her mind. "I'll take it."

"Hallelujah," said Jody. "Now, all we need to get you is some shoes."

"Good thing the shops are closing." Dusty went back into the change rooms.

"You forget... the shops are open all day tomorrow. All. Day. Dusty. Isn't that great."

"Great?" Her headache intensified at the idea. "You know I'm meant to be relaxing?"

"You would be if you weren't fighting about what clothes to buy. I have good taste."

Dusty opened the curtain with the dress in hand. She felt more comfortable back in her jeans and T-shirt. "But it's not my taste."

"No. But this dress suits you, not you suiting the dress."

"Come on, let's get the dress, get something to eat, and then go home. I'm too tired for this anymore."

Dusty put the dress on the counter. She had another few days with her sister, a dinner with Blaise, and a headache that was fast turning into a migraine.

All she wanted to do was to get this all over so that she could return to the farm.

DUSTY SLEPT in the next morning until nearly midday. She couldn't believe it. The noise of the traffic had been keeping her awake so she opted to use earplugs. The silence soothed her into a long, deep sleep. One she hadn't had for a long time.

She rolled over lazily contemplating going back to sleep and nestled the pillow under her shoulder. Dusty decided she could stay like this all day. She couldn't remember the last time she managed to sleep in.

Something moved at the end of the bed. Any hope

of going to sleep left her as she sat up and saw Jody's cat trying to claim space at the end of the bed.

"Oi, get off." Dusty spoke louder than normal because of the earplugs. The cat just looked at her and dug its claws into the quilt. Dusty groaned in annoyance and reached forward to push the cat off the bed. "Go away."

The cat pushed back.

"You're sleeping in her spot, Dusty," said Jody as she peeked into the room. "Don't be so harsh on her."

"Kitty, I've claimed this bed." Dusty reached forward, and the cat jumped off the bed.

"You've hurt her feelings," said Jody. She reached down and picked up Kitty and gave her a cuddle.

"You didn't let her in by any chance?" asked Dusty.

"You don't have to yell."

Dusty took out the earplugs. "You did let her in, didn't you?"

Jody kissed the top of Kitty's head. "Course not. Now, come on, sleepy head, we've got to get to the shops and sort out shoes for you. Then I'm going to do your hair. We've got a big day ahead, which is really only half a day because you slept so much."

Dusty sat up on the bed. "I do remember when you're on the farm you seem to sleep the day away."

"That's 'cause there's nothing to do there."

Dusty gasped in mock horror. "I can always do with extra help. There's plenty of jobs that need to be done. Besides, you don't come home that much these days."

"Are you having a go at me?" Jody narrowed her eyes.

"No." Dusty stood up. "Just miss having you around."

"We're chalk and cheese and fought like cats and dogs growing up. I'm not sure why you'd miss me."

Dusty shrugged her shoulders. "I guess I remember the good times."

"Like that time we played in the rain and used the roses as confetti and Mom went ape at us?"

"Yes. Though I think you're the first person I've met who you *can* take the country out of."

"I don't think I ever had the country in me." Jody let Kitty jump down and reclaimed the bed.

"Maybe a little?"

"Not like you anyway. You love it."

Dusty looked at the cat as it jumped back on the bed. "You didn't take long."

"Leave her alone, you're traumatizing her." Kitty kneaded the quilt into place making her movements clear she wasn't happy with the current situation. "Yep, well, I hate the city. At least we've found our place in the world."

"Even though you think I should visit more?"

"Yes, but I get why you don't." Dusty slipped on some socks to keep her feet warm.

"I can make a deal, you visit me more, and I'll visit you."

"That could work."

"I reckon it would, especially if you end up dating that Blaise guy."

"Oi." Dusty punched Jody's arm. "There's nothing between us."

"You know I know that there is." Jody rubbed her arm. "Which is why you better hurry up and have something to eat, so we can finish getting your outfit for tonight."

"I got the dress last night, what else do I need to be getting?"

"Shoes for starters. Your feet are a size smaller than mine."

"Can't afford it." She walked down the narrow hallway of the two-bedroom apartment her sister rented.

"We're going Op shopping." Jody followed her sister to the kitchen.

"I'm not sure I want to wear someone else's shoes." She pulled out two slices of bread and put them in the toaster.

"Come on, it'll be fun. Besides, do you even own any heels?"

Dusty shook her head.

"Well, it's about time you got some, and I think we could also find some other clothes for you. Something other than the usual jeans and striped shirts that you're always wearing."

"I've got T-shirts, too."

"Yeah, one's with bull horns on them. We're going to get you some variety."

"We don't need to go shopping anyway. I'm going to cancel tonight. This is all turning into a much bigger deal than I wanted it to be."

"You can't."

"I can."

"But you asked him to dinner."

"Yeah, well, I've changed my mind." Dusty set the kettle to boil.

"You're chicken."

Her sister was right, she was. All she was thinking was a simple pub meal, but now Blaise was picking her up, and Jody was encouraging her to wear a dress to impress him, and well, that wasn't quite what she had in mind. She did have thoughts of getting him naked, but she wasn't planning on acting on them. They'd tried, gotten way too close that afternoon in the shearing shed, and well, she didn't think the relationship could be patched up. She was just being kind, returning the favor. After all, he'd done the books for them, so she thought of this more like a business dinner.

"I can't make any promises." Dusty didn't want to go shopping again. But she did want to spend some time with her sister. "You think there's nothing to do at the farm, but there's nothing to do here. Just shopping, shopping, shopping."

"Well, we could go to the beach, but you've already

told me that the beach back home is so much better even though there always seems to be jellyfish there."

"They aren't stingers, so don't worry."

"We can go out for lunch, but both of us are cash poor."

"True."

"We can go to the museums, but I'm not sure that's your thing."

"How about the movies?" The toast popped up and Dusty juggled them to the plate and started to smear them with margarine and Vegemite. They didn't have a cinema back at Wilkton. There used to be a drive-in, but it had closed down. If she wanted to watch a movie, she could download it from Foxstar or be old-fashioned and go into town and rent a DVD, but that was a problem when it had to be returned the next day, and she didn't go into town every day.

"What about tomorrow?"

"Then I can meet this mysterious man of yours."

"Maybe."

"What do you mean maybe?"

"Depends. If you don't go out with Blaise tonight, then you don't get to meet Ethan."

Dusty put her hands on her hips and glared at her sister. "You drive a hard bargain."

It wasn't what she wanted to agree to. She weighed up the options in her head, trying to work out how much she didn't want to see Blaise to how much she wanted to meet Ethan. "Fine."

"Good. Now hurry up, we leave in fifteen minutes."

"You take much longer than that to get ready. You were always hours in the bathroom on the farm."

"I have more energy in the city, thirteen minutes now." Jody left the room.

Dusty finished eating her toast and then got herself a glass of orange juice. The good thing about getting up so late was that she could have breakfast and lunch at once. Every time she thought of Blaise, a shiver went through her body, and she became flustered. After all, she wanted a second chance with him, but now that it was happening, she was nervous as hell.

It's just a business dinner.

She knew she was kidding herself.

Somehow things had gone way beyond that.

Dusty managed to have a two-minute shower and pull on her usual jeans and T-shirt with a black jacket and dress boots and be ready before Jody was.

"Are you ready yet?" Dusty yelled from the spare room.

"Five minutes."

That's what her sister always said when they were getting ready to go out when growing up. She usually always needed more than five minutes. At least, she was out of the bathroom now, so she shouldn't be too much longer.

Her stomach twisted with nerves about the evening ahead. Dusty decided that she'd text Blaise now and cancel. If she rang then, she wouldn't hold her nerve. His soft voice would make her go all woozy, and she was sure he'd be able to convince her to come. She hated this waiting, her mind kept making this into a bigger deal than it needed to be, and Jody wasn't helping either.

Dusty went through her bag but couldn't find her phone. In a panic, she tipped everything onto the bed causing Kitty to run away hissing at her. Dusty sorted through the items, her purse was there, but she couldn't find her phone.

It must be stolen. She rushed out into the kitchen, searched around there, but it wasn't on the table, or the bench, and then she looked in the lounge room. *Maybe it's in the ute?* Dusty went outside and searched the ute but couldn't find it. A sinking, knotted feeling spread out from her stomach.

Stolen. It must be.

But they hadn't taken her purse, so it wasn't quite adding up.

She was trying to remember when she last had the phone. She'd looked at it last night when they were shopping and spent a bit of time trying to decode a message from her mom. She swore she'd put it back in her handbag.

"Jody, Jody." She ran back inside the apartment.

"What?" Jody was finally dressed in a colorful skirt made from about three different types of material and a black long-sleeved top.

"I've been robbed. I can't find my phone." Dusty puffed as she talked.

Jody laughed.

"I don't see what's so funny." Dusty glared at her sister.

"Be honest, Dusty. Why do you want your phone?"

A flood of heat rose to Dusty's face. She wasn't about to tell Jody the truth. "To ring Mom and make sure that she's all right."

"Yeah, right."

"It's true."

"I don't believe you. I think you were going to ring Blaise and cancel tonight's dinner."

"Was not." She wasn't going to ring, she was going to text—it was a minor detail.

"You were going to be a chicken and text him, right?"

Dusty swallowed her words.

"Huh, I'm right."

"I'm not admitting anything."

"I've got your phone."

"What?" Dusty didn't know whether to be relieved or angry. "What are you doing with my phone?"

"Stopping you from making a stupid mistake and canceling dinner tonight."

"It's my choice."

"Yes. I think you're overcome with nerves, and you're going to take the easy way out and not go."

"So, you took my phone? Give it back."

"You can have it back when you go to dinner with Blaise and not before."

"What if I have an important phone call?"

"Well, I'll worry about that *if* it happens." Jody picked up her handbag. "Are you ready?"

Dusty nodded.

"Well, let's go then." Jody grabbed her sister's hand and pulled her to the door. "We're going to have some fun."

Dusty groaned as if she was in pain. Her idea of fun was very different to what Jody thought was fun.

This was going to be a trying afternoon.

CHAPTER 20

"LEAVE YOUR DRESS ALONE," said Jody as Dusty fidgeted while they waited in the lounge room for Blaise to arrive.

Dusty made a frustrated sound as she stood up and started walking around the room. She knew this wasn't just a dinner meal. She'd only been saying that to stop herself from getting too nervous. Based on how things went for them in the past, there was a real likelihood that things would go pear-shaped. They hadn't disagreed on anything when they met at the coffee shop. *Maybe it could work?*

"Relax. You keep saying that it's just a business dinner." Jody flipped through the television stations.

"So, when is Ethan getting here?"

"After you've gone."

A car door slammed outside, and Dusty held her breath.

Jody let out a squeal of excitement, switched the television to mute and went to peek between the blinds. "It's him."

The doorbell rang, and Dusty took a deep breath and opened the door before Jody had the chance to. She saw Blaise's jaw drop, and he just stared at her. Dusty blushed.

Blaise whistled. "You look great."

Dusty soaked up his response, her cheeks flushed hotter. *Glad I got this dress.* She shut the door behind her.

"Have a good time," yelled her sister.

"So, where are we going?" asked Dusty.

"You'll find out." Blaise stepped aside to let her walk in front of him.

Dusty chewed her bottom lip as she walked to his car. She had to concentrate as she walked, the second-hand pair of black shoes only had a small heel, but it was much higher than she was used to.

Blaise opened his car door for her. Dusty couldn't believe how clean his car was. Her ute always had a layer of dirt in the interior, and on the passenger's side was a small metal bucket that held various farm tools. Here, she could stretch out her feet and the floor was clean, not stained with oil or mud. It was like she'd stepped into another world. The door clicked quietly close, and Blaise got into the driver's seat.

"I love your car," said Dusty.

Blaise started up the car. Dusty could barely hear

the engine, and when he changed gears, it was smooth and effortless.

"I'd imagine it's much easier to drive than the tractors and trucks you're used to," said Blaise.

"Are you going to let me know where we're going to have dinner?"

"No, just into the city."

Dusty held her breath. It was worse being in the passenger's seat when driving in the city. The cars were so close, she was sure they were going to hit them. All the lights made her almost forget it was dark out. She was so used to driving with only her headlights showing the way. But here, there were so many more lights and different colors—red, orange, and green. She felt a headache coming along and didn't know how Blaise could be so calm while driving with so many distractions.

Blaise parked his car on the side of the road. "The restaurant is just down the road here."

Before Dusty could get out, Blaise had gotten out and opened the door for her. Dusty was beginning to feel like this was more of a date. *Why did I have to ask him out to dinner?* But she had to admit, the attention was stirring a hot heat inside of her, and she had to concentrate on keeping her breathing steady.

They walked down to the street, and Blaise opened the door to a local pub. *Blackbirds*.

Dusty expelled a long breath. A pub meal was something she could cope with. But when she walked inside, this hotel had a modern feel and was decorated to look more upscale. *It looks expensive.*

"This way." Blaise led her down the hallway into the dining area which was set with an old Victorian-like decoration. The tables all had white tablecloths, and there was new carpet on the floor. This was nothing like the pubs back home.

A waiter approached them. "Blaise, how are you?"

"Good, thanks, mate." They shook hands. "This is Dusty."

"Pleased to meet you," said the waiter. "I'm Scott, Blaise's younger brother. Welcome to my pub."

"Oh, I didn't know you had a brother." And one that owned a pub. Dusty didn't know what to say. This was too much to process all at once.

"What, Blaise hasn't mentioned me?" His tone was jovial.

"Well…" started Dusty, but the rest of the words caught in her throat.

"I've got a nice romantic table for two for you."

Scott winked at Dusty and showed them the way to a small booth on the other side of the room.

Scott placed the white cloth napkin on Dusty's lap and was going to do the same to Blaise, but he stopped him.

"I can do this."

"Blaise, really, it's all part of the service. Can I get you some drinks?"

"How about some filtered water and the wine list."

"Okay." He left them.

"You've taken me to your brother's pub?" The words finally came out.

Business dinner my ass.

"He owns part of this restaurant."

"Oh. Impressive."

"Don't worry about the price, we can go Dutch if you like."

"Dutch?" She played with the edge of the napkin on her lap.

"Pay for our own meals." He smiled gently.

Her internal butterflies took off in flight, tickling her belly. She couldn't think of anything else except wanting to kiss his lips. "Oh, but I'm meant to be paying."

"I guess I'm saying you don't have to."

"But I want to. Unless the prices are going to be really, really high." She couldn't believe she just said that.

"I'm not sure what you think is expensive."

Scott returned with some filtered water and filled their glasses. "Here's the wine list." He handed it to Blaise. "The specials are written on the board over there." He left them to think and went to seat another couple.

"White or red?" asked Blaise.

"White," said Dusty. She hoped that a bottle wouldn't cost too much. Maybe she'd have to take him up on the offer to pay for his meal. "Can I look?"

Blaise handed over the wine list. "Lady's choice."

Dusty looked at the list. Her eyes widened as she saw the prices.

"Like I said, you don't have to pay." His voice was gentle and caused her butterflies to set off in all directions. "It could be my peace offering to you. Or, if you're willing... I can pay, and we can call this a date."

Dusty took a deep breath. *A date.* It certainly was what this was. Based on how she felt right now, this wasn't about business, this was a date through and through. "Okay."

"Really?" Blaise looked surprised.

"Yes, but I'll pay for the wine only because you've done a great job with our tax return."

"Deal, and I'm glad to be taking you on a date, Dusty."

His smile deepened as he looked at her. Her skin flushed under his gaze, and she tried to control herself because, right now, she wanted to lean over and kiss him. She didn't want to hold back anymore. Blaise made her feel a certain way—safe, protected, and admired. A flood of emotions emerged from inside of her. *Get a grip.*

"Me, too," said Dusty.

She looked back at the wine list before she lost control and cleared the table so she could reach him and kiss him hard on the lips. "What do you think of a Sauvignon Semillon?"

"A good choice."

Blaise lifted his hand, and his brother came over and took the wine order. In no time at all, he was back with the bottle.

"You're organized," said Dusty.

Back home, she'd have to go to the bar to order, and it could take a long time.

"Have to be on my toes. If the customers aren't happy, then there's plenty of other places for them to eat," said Scott.

She looked through the menu and nearly died at the prices. "You eat like this all the time?"

Blaise laughed, gently, not a judgmental laugh that she'd been used to from Aaron. "Yes, living in the city comes at a price."

"I don't know how you do it."

"Well, I'm actually thinking of taking my business to Wilkton"

Dusty choked. "That's a big change from out of nowhere."

"Someone pushed me into that direction."

She looked at him and couldn't help think that someone was *her*. "I didn't mean to say what I did after we had..."

"I know. And don't worry about it. I'm treating this night as a new slate for us. We've both made some mistakes, so how about we forget them and get to know each other?"

"Agreed." Dusty felt the knots in her stomach

easing. She lifted her glass of wine. "To getting to know each other."

"Here, here."

They clicked their glasses to the evening ahead.

"You know, now that this is a date, we could order something different," said Blaise.

"I'm a meat-and-three-veggie kind of girl. I'm not sure about eating anything too different." Blaise had a way of easing her out of her comfort zone which both excited her but made her nervous at the same time. "Anything else is probably wasted on me."

"What about oysters?" He raised one of his eyebrows to make sure she got the meaning he was suggesting.

Dusty giggled. "Only as a starter."

Blaise smiled. "I've got a chef's sampling menu in mind."

"Sounds expensive."

"I know the boss, mate's rates. How does this sound... seven dishes I can guarantee will blow your mind in taste and flavor?"

Oh yeah, I want you to be blowing my mind but not with food. Dusty cleared her throat and looked at him with big eyes. "I'll try anything once."

"Just the once?"

"Well, sometimes I'll go in for seconds." She raised her eyebrow at him.

"Good, because I'm relying on that."

A heat flushed deep within Dusty. She hadn't realized how much fun she could have with him. "Makes two of us."

She could be just as cheeky, and her comment was rewarded with a huge smile from Blaise. Plus, she could see his cheeks turning a soft pink. It made him look adorable.

"Hate to interrupt whatever you two are blushing about, but what would you like to order?" Scott looked calm and collected even though the place was beginning to get busy.

"I'm not going red," said Blaise indignantly.

Scott looked at Dusty. She laughed. "You're turning red."

"Thanks, guys." Blaise wrinkled his forehead, pretending to be annoyed at them both. "Is there anything you won't eat?"

Dusty shook her head. *I'd even take a bite of you.*

"Two degustations and make them your best, sir."

"Excellent choice." Scott turned to Dusty. "You won't be disappointed."

He left them, and in no time the palate cleanser, strawberry sorbet in a flute with some French champagne, came out.

"This is quite something," said Dusty as she had a mouthful of sorbet.

"Nothing like French champagne."

Dusty's eyebrows raised in surprise. "French?"

Blaise nodded.

Dusty felt nervous since the most expensive dinner

she'd ever had was a pub meal. She had never had a reason to eat expensive food, and her mom was a good cook.

"Scallops with nori and konbu butter on a tatsoi salad," said Scott as he placed a dish in front of Dusty.

Dusty hadn't heard half of the ingredients before and just looked at the tiny amount of food that was on her plate. "You sure this is going to fill me up?"

"After seven of these dishes, yes, you'll be stuffed."

Dusty looked at the different sizes of forks to her left and wondered which one to pick up. Her hands trembled. "I didn't know there could be more than one fork. I mean a fork is just a fork." Her stomach tightened.

"Just take whichever one you want." His voice had a soothing effect on her.

Dusty noticed he took one from the outside and copied. Dusty took a bite and closed her eyes as the flavor absorbed through her tongue. "Oh my God."

"I'd hoped you'd be saying that."

She opened her eyes, and Blaise winked at her. She crossed her legs to try and keep her abdominal muscles from contracting. The banter with Blaise was setting her ablaze.

"I hope they bring out the oyster. They do this Asian style soup in a shot glass with the oyster inside."

"You like oysters." Dusty wasn't so sure about the sound of an oyster in a shot glass, but if it was as good as the scallop, then she wasn't about to complain.

"I only like the side effects."

"Well, you're on fire tonight." Dusty fanned herself with her hands.

"Oh, shall I turn down the heat level a bit, then?"

"Hell, no."

Blaise caught Scott as he walked past to make sure they were given the oyster dish.

"The things you do for family," said Scott. But he delivered the shot glasses himself. "This is an added dish, so I hope you have room for eight."

"Amazing." Dusty tapped the edge of the napkin in the corners of her mouth after she'd swallowed the oyster. "I've not had anything like that before."

"There's plenty more to come."

"Careful, you're building up expectations now."

Blaise laughed. "I plan to follow through."

"So, did you get that promotion?" Dusty decided while she didn't want to reduce the heat, she needed to, otherwise she'd start ripping off his shirt, right here, right now.

"After hitting Aaron, what do you think?"

"I'm sorry."

"Not your fault."

"Sort of is, maybe indirectly. Anyway, he's long out of the picture."

"Good."

"So, no promotion then?"

Blaise shook his head. "I got something much better."

"What?"

"I've started up my own business."

"Good."

"I've got a few clients down your way, so I'll be down your end of the world more regularly."

Dusty liked the sound of that. "Is it going well?"

"Yes, but slow. I've had to make a lot of allowances and take a big wage cut, but the business is growing, and I believe I'll come out on top."

"You like being on top."

"Of course, so do you." He looked at her intensely causing Dusty to blush.

"Sorry to disturb you. Here we have crisp fried tea-smoked duck, choy sum, blood orange, and tamarind mousse," said Scott.

"Smells delicious," said Dusty.

She no longer cared if she didn't know the ingredients. The food was bringing her tastebuds alive, just as Blaise's stare was causing waves of pleasure to ripple through her body.

The seven-course meal came out over about four hours, and Dusty was amazed at the flavors of food each time and the intricacy of the dishes. She lost herself in the conversation with Blaise and his beautiful eyes that always felt like they were embracing her each time he looked at her.

When Dusty thought there were no more dishes coming out, Scott delivered petite fours and dessert wine. "For the lovebirds."

Dusty bit her lip to say they weren't lovebirds, even though she glowed from the attention Blaise was giving her. More like the conversation they'd been having. She hoped the people at the tables nearby hadn't heard. But really, she didn't care. It was like everyone else faded away leaving just her and Blaise. *It's the wine*, she kidded to herself. But she knew it wasn't.

The longer the evening and the more time that they spent with each other, the harder it was to keep control and not kiss Blaise in public.

They ended the night with a coffee, and Scott had to come over to kick them out because they were closing. "Come on, you two, some of us actually want to get home tonight." He raised his eyebrows at them both as he put up the last of the chairs on the table next to them.

"Okay, okay, bring me the bill," said Blaise.

"Don't forget, I'm paying for the wine." Dusty clamped her mouth shut. She was just a little tipsy, not too much, only a little, but it was like her mouth was in its own gear. She'd already made that point a thousand times. She felt at ease with Blaise and had completely relaxed.

"I'll drop you home," said Blaise.

He took her hand in his, his warmth eased up her arm and though her body causing her muscles to shudder. Going back home to her sister's was the last thing she wanted to do right now. She hated to admit it, but she wanted Blaise, naked and in bed with her.

She got into the car, and Blaise drove her back to her sister's place. This time she didn't care about the traffic or the lights. All she could think of was getting Blaise naked and into bed.

Dusty took a deep breath to try and expel some of the sexual tension building inside of her. *One step at a time*, she tried to remind herself. They'd already followed the path of lust, and now, as much as she wanted to go down that path, she also wanted a serious relationship.

"I don't think I've ever had a meal that lasted that long or was that delicious," said Dusty.

"I'm glad you liked it."

Blaise parked the car at her sister's and turned off the engine. Dusty's heart galloped in her chest.

"I had a great time." He reached over and brushed a piece of her hair that had come loose. Her body shivered pleasantly from his touch.

"Me, too," she answered. She held her breath as he leaned over and kissed her on the lips, transferring a fire to her mouth that shot down her body and was caught by her clenching thighs. He kissed her again. Another blaze of fire went through her body, and she groaned in pleasure.

God, I want more. Something about him made her feel alive—his touch, his salty lips, his boyish features, and his muscles. Her mouth moved with his quietly urging him for more.

He pulled back from her and held her chin with his finger. "You're one hell of a woman." His finger slipped off the edge of her chin, and she looked into his blue eyes and felt a passionate heat radiating from out, mesmerizing her.

Blaise got out of the car and went around to the passenger's side. Dusty thought she was about to explode if things didn't go any further. She was happy to rip off his shirt and get to know his toned chest muscles once more.

Dusty took his hand and stepped out of the car.

"I'll walk you to the door."

He slipped his arm around her waist, and they stepped up the dark driveway to the apartment at the back. She noticed that her sister's car wasn't in the carport, and she was relieved to see her ute still in the visitor's car park.

"Would you mind if I saw you tomorrow?" asked Blaise.

His gentleman persona was adding to the tension building between her thighs. She turned to face him, and he kept his arm around her waist. "I'd be disappointed if I didn't see you."

He kissed her again. Slow and long. She lost herself in his taste and softness as his hand moved up under her dress along her skin, and she pushed hard into his body wanting more. "How about we have breakfast?"

He made a positive sound and moved his lips down along her neck, kissing her softly, almost like nibbles that sent her skin on fire. He picked her up from the ground and leaned back gripping her buttocks tightly. He returned her to the ground gracefully, keeping his hands under her skirt, his fingers now exploring the pattern of her lace knickers and the elastic edge, toying with the option of slipping under another layer.

"Let's go inside," he mumbled between kissing her.

"Hell, yeah."

Dusty wriggled out of his embrace long enough to get the keys out of her handbag. His hands slipped around her waist, and he kissed the back of her neck while she fumbled opening the security door, then the main door.

Dusty barely managed to have closed and locked the door before Blaise grabbed her and pulled her close to him and kissed her hard with hungry intent. She kissed him back, dropping the keys on the floor, then her handbag, and holding him tight around his shoulders. He pushed his hips against her, and she felt his cock hard and ready.

Dusty tugged at his jacket, which he helped to shrug off. They turned around, moving a step at a time further into the apartment, but they kept being distracted by each other.

Dusty didn't want to stop kissing his lips or feeling his body against hers, and she wanted the skin- on-skin contact. She started unbuttoning his shirt as his hands slipped under her dress, skimming along her skin upward in search of her jewel. She lifted her leg up around his waist, and he pulled her in closer, keeping a firm grip on her.

In the heat of the moment, Dusty ripped open his shirt, buttons flew outward dropping on the wooden floor, her hands were now rewarded with the smooth warmth of his skin. They stepped around each other moving slowly toward the bedroom.

He reached up and unzipped her dress, easing it down over her shoulders causing her to be pinned temporarily and at his mercy as he kissed around her breasts, biting the exposed skin with his lips and licking off her salty flavor. She kept her leg around his waist, and his hands slipped up her dress again and then slapped her hard. She groaned as an electric wave of pleasure shot up her body, and she clenched her thighs wishing he was already in her and she had something there to hold on to.

Dusty wriggled her arms and her dress fell away. She pulled off his shirt as he pushed her against the wall in the hallway, sliding his hands down her back sending her skin prickling and her chest aching for more.

This time, he unclasped her bra and cupped one breast. He squeezed it while he put his mouth over her other nipple and flicked it with his tongue. She leaned her head back and groaned, almost losing herself in the pleasure from his touch. But she kept her mind, just, and dipped her hands below his waist, gliding down to hold him. He pulsed under her touch and moaned.

She undid his trousers pushing them to the floor. He stepped out of them as she pulled down his jocks, going down on her knees. Then she took his hard cock in her mouth for a few stokes while he moaned and stiffened even more. Only wanting to tease him, she slowly stood up kissing him up along his belly, then chest and finally finding his mouth.

As their lips touched again, a new wave of intense heat flashed down her body. He pulled down her lacy knickers dropping on his knees, kissed her, his tongue flicking between her folds. She rested against the wall for support not wanting him to stop. Her hands moved in over his head, gliding through his dark hair as he stayed on his knees kissing her until her body shuddered.

While she was coming down from the heights of pleasure, he stood and kissed her lips. Played with her nipples which sent her back on the waves of bliss. She still felt him hard against her, and the passion began to intensify again between them.

Blaise lifted her up and took her into the bedroom playfully dropping her on the bed. The cat hissed and ran out of the room, leaving them giggling. He picked up the condom packet that was by the nightstand. "Hopeful?"

Dusty didn't remember putting that there, but she didn't care.

"What's taking you so long?"

She smiled and took hold of his cock, moving her hand up and down keeping him extra hard as he pulled off the wrapper, then eased himself on the bed next to her. She quickly straddled him. He placed his hands around her hips and looked at her with a hungry pleasure. She moved to bring him closer, and then with control she didn't think she had, slowly slid his cock into her. They groaned together, and he arched his hips forward. Keeping the rhythm slow, she moved back and forth fighting the urge to go faster. She felt herself rising with him, and she couldn't help but go faster as they reached their peak together, exploding in groans and gasps. She flopped down on top of him, and he buried his face in her neck holding her tight for a moment.

Dusty rolled off of him, her skin sweaty, prickled with pleasure. She snuggled next to him, puffing together as they floated back down to earth in each other's arms.

"That... that... was..." puffed Dusty, but she couldn't get the words out as Blaise kissed her softly and lightly on her lips.

"Yes, and I think in a little while maybe we can... you know..."

Dusty giggled at the thought of going another round. "Long night ahead, then."

"Only if you're up to it."

She rolled on top of him and pinned down his arms. "Only if you are."

He smiled, then reached up and kissed her forcing her backward.

THE NOISE of the neighbor reversing their car out woke Dusty. It took a moment for her to realize where she was and that last night Blaise and she had been at it for hours. With little sleep, she was amazed at how awake she actually felt. The clock flashed eleven.

She rolled over and Blaise opened his eyes.

"Morning," she said shyly.

He reached his arm around her and pulled her into a close cuddle. "Morning." He kissed her.

Dusty lay silent in his arms, enjoying the movement, and not wanting to ruin the moment by speaking. But sooner or later, they were going to have to get up. And worse. Then have the conversation about what they were going to do next. She didn't want to bring it up yet, but it was going to be unavoidable soon.

"How about we go out for brunch," said Blaise lazily running his finger along the side of her body.

"Okay." She kissed him. "But that means we have to get up."

"I know." He pulled her on top of him. "I guess we have to get up eventually."

They kissed some more delaying the inevitable start of the day.

"Probably should get up, my sister's bound to come home soon," said Dusty. "Want a shower?"

"Only with you."

Dusty laughed. "Fine with me."

She tried to roll away, but he held her tight around the waist stopping her from going anywhere. They tussled for a moment before Blaise gave in and let her go.

"I'll go and get you a towel."

Dusty ran off before being tackled again, down to the linen closet and pulled out a towel. Out the corner of her eye, she saw something on the kitchen table. *My phone.* She picked it up and saw she had a new message.

> Hope you guys had a good night. Let me know when you're done ;)

Dusty's face reddened reading the text from her sister. *That's who left the condom on the nightstand.*

She should've known. Her sister was assuming way too much and yet she was right.

"What's taking you so long?" Blaise walked into the kitchen, naked.

"Nothing."

He walked up behind her and slipped his hands around her waist and looked at the phone. "Oh yeah, we're going to be a while yet." He started nibbling at the back of her neck, and she was about to push him away, but then he slipped his hand between her thighs and found her spot, and all she could do was lean back and enjoy.

"Yeah, we're going to be a while," she answered.

CHAPTER 21

"WHERE DO you want to go and eat?" asked Dusty after they managed to shower and dress. Dusty, at least, had the comfortable option of being able to put on her jeans and T-shirt, but Blaise had to put on his dinner clothes again, and of course, he couldn't do up his shirt.

"Let's go to the city," said Blaise as he tried to get his shirt to sit flat.

They had managed to find all but one of the buttons and Dusty offered to stitch them back on, but Blaise didn't want to do that. "We can go back via my home first and then into the city."

"You sure, or we can just have something simple here."

"I don't want to let you out of my sight for a little while, not now we've finally managed to get this far."

"You'll have to let me out of your sight soon enough."

"Just not yet." He kissed her. A fresh warmth flowed into Dusty's body. *I can get used to this.*

"I have to go home tomorrow, you know," said Dusty.

"Do you have to go back tomorrow?" He kept his hands around her.

"No... yes..." She didn't want to leave the workload with her mom. Seeding was done, the ewes had lambed, she could stay here a week. "If I stayed for a bit, then what?"

"I could come down to you for a while."

"What about your business?"

"I can use the internet and the phone. I'd just have to make sure I'm connected to a service with better coverage, but these are all details that are easy to work out because I know what I want." He looked at Dusty as they walked out of the apartment to his car. "I want you."

A ripple of pleasure ran through her body, sending her skin hot and electrified. "Do you want me for now, or longer?"

"Longer. But you know we've got to set the foundation first. Give it a go and see what happens." Blaise started his car.

"I know. So, if I stay a week, then maybe you could come to the farm for a week?"

For Dusty, it seemed surreal to be talking about this as they drove through the streets. "How do you think you'll cope with farm life?"

"You're planning on working me to the bone, are you?"

Dusty laughed.

"You are, aren't you?" He winked at her. "I'm on to you."

"There might be times when I need your help."

"The way I think I see it is that you don't need me to help you all the time to run the farm. You do that very well."

Dusty blushed from the compliment. Not many guys thought she ran the farm well, and it was always an uphill battle with them trying to stop them from taking over.

"I can help out when you need it, but otherwise I'll be busy running my own business. I think that would be better, otherwise we'd get in each other's way too much."

Dusty exhaled slowly and felt her chest ease. Suddenly, it was like she no longer had to battle with Blaise, that whatever was annoying them before had gone. *All to do with last night, I'm sure.* She flushed at the reminder of their time together.

"I'm not good at doing this without being in control."

"I know." He pulled up in front of a house in Unley.

"But I'll give it a go."

She wanted another chance with this guy, and she got it, and so far, things were hot and great and who knows what this could turn into. Her stomach fluttered, just a little, but a good flutter mixed with excitement and nerves. She knew for sure she'd give this a go with him.

"I'm glad." He got out of the car. "You can come in if you like."

Dusty got out and followed him into his house. She was sure this was going to take longer than Blaise just changing his shirt. Once inside and with him taking his clothes off, she was sure she'd have to pounce on him again. "You live here alone?"

"Yes, I like being with others, but I like my own space, too." He unlocked the door and walked in. "It's a bit hard to pay the mortgage now that I've got my own business."

"Rent back in Wilkton would be cheaper for you."

"Yeah, it's an option to rent this place out."

"Why don't you?"

"Because I've caught myself a little dust cloud," said Blaise.

He caught Dusty by the waist, pulled her in close to him, and kissed her soft and deep.

They stayed at his place a lot longer than it took to change a shirt. And then after another shower, they finally made it back into the car and Blaise drove them into the city.

Dusty took out her phone. "Oh no." There were about five missed calls and ten messages.

"What?"

"Something must be wrong."

She'd never had this many messages on her phone before, except the time when her dad passed away. They were all from her sister.

Are you OK?

I'm calling the police if you don't answer.

"OH, NO."

"Something has gone wrong?"

"Yeah, I haven't let my sister know I'm okay."

She typed a quick message saying she was fine, don't call the police, and she was going into the city with Blaise for something to eat. And she was looking forward to seeing Jody's new boyfriend now that she had gone out last night.

Her sister typed back saying she'd meet them in the city when they were done.

"You don't mind seeing my sister again, do you?" asked Dusty.

This was like a few months into the relationship

when other family members were introduced. Dusty felt a little unsure about bringing Blaise into her life so quickly. She looked at him concentrating as he drove. He was lovely, sweet, strong, and suddenly she didn't care as long as he was hers.

"That's fine."

They went to a café on Rundle Street, and when they were nearly finished eating, Dusty had texted her sister to let them know where they were. It didn't take long for Jody to find them.

"I thought you guys were never going to find the phone," said Jody as she walked into the café.

"You were assuming too much," said Dusty hoping she wasn't turning red. "You didn't know what we were going to do."

"No, but I decided to hope for the best."

"You were always the optimist."

"It's good to see you two together, anyway." She sat down, and a guy sat down next to her. "I'm happy to take full credit."

"I'm not so sure that's the reality," said Dusty.

She looked over at Blaise. This was such a bad idea bringing him here to have brunch with her sister and boyfriend, especially so early in their relationship. *Is that what we have, a relationship?* She looked over to the guy who was looking awkward with his big black glasses. "Ethan?"

"Yes."

He was well groomed, a typical modern city boy. At least Blaise had some earthiness hidden under his expensive clothes. Maybe that was one of the things that attracted him to her. *One of the many things.* After only twenty-four hours, the list was suddenly getting longer. She was determined to take it only one step at a time. Dusty could just imagine them trying to do the accounts without ripping each other's clothes off. She tried to suppress a smile.

"So, are you guys still up for a movie?"

"I don't know."

She was beginning to get nervous without having the chance to talk with Blaise about what they were going to do from here. Well, they had plenty of time this morning, but chose to spend it another way. And she wasn't about to start complaining about that.

"What are you going to see?" asked Blaise.

"Dusty's choice."

"I don't know what's showing."

"As long as it's not a chick flick," said Blaise. He took a sip of his coffee.

"Well, there's only one thing to do, we will have to go and have a look," said Jody.

"Okay," said Dusty.

"If you guys want to be alone, then we don't mind."

"No, it's okay," said Blaise.

Dusty wasn't sure if a movie was a good idea or not.

But by the time they decided on a movie and were

sitting in the dark, Blaise on her right, holding her hand, Dusty thought this was the best idea and had to keep reminding herself this was really happening. Simply holding hands was a beautiful end to a wild night.

CHAPTER 22

BLAISE TAPED up the box in his home and scribbled 'Kitchen' on the top with a black marker. He couldn't believe he was doing this. He hadn't even told Dusty. He was going to surprise her by moving to Wilkton, so they could at least be closer and to give their relationship a real chance.

Blaise stretched his neck before taking another flattened box and taping it into shape. He felt lost without seeing her for nearly a month, and the phone messages and emailing wasn't nearly enough. Blaise wanted to be spending the evenings with her, cooking dinner since she couldn't cook, which he'd found out the hard way. Curling up together on the lounge and watching a movie sounded like the perfect way to spend an evening with the woman he'd fallen in love with.

"Hey, are you ready to load up the truck?" asked his

mate, Simon, as he walked into the kitchen. Simon had a small truck license and offered his skills to Blaise to help move his things to the country.

"Nearly." Blaise had gotten behind in the last of the packing up and still had a few cupboards in the kitchen to do. His stomach twisted. *Am I doing the right thing?* He'd agonized over what to do, but there was a deep force driving him, making him want to be with Dusty and not waste any more time thinking about whether or not it was a going to work. When they saw each other over the last few months, it worked. That was all that he needed to know. Blaise scrunched up a sheet of newspaper and began packing the pots and pans.

"Come on, man, no need to get sentimental."

Blaise threw a ball of scrunched-up newspaper at him. Simon ducked and the paper easily missed him.

"I can't believe you're going out bush," said Simon. "I think you need your head checked."

"That's love for you," said Simon as he came in carrying a box from another room. "Come on, Blaise, we've got a long trip ahead. We have to get back to Adelaide by dark otherwise we have to pay for another day for the use of the truck that's just going to be sitting in the driveway."

"I know. I know. I thought you guys were meant to be helping me."

"We are. We've got some beers in the truck already," said Simon.

He picked up the box Blaise just finished sealing and groaned from the weight.

"You need to work out more," said Blaise.

"Yeah, right," said Simon as he straightened up and walked outside to the truck trying not to strain under the weight. "You've packed too much in this one."

Blaise rubbed his eyes. They were dry from the long hours he was working and from having to pack up his house. While dating Dusty over the last few months, he'd gained more clients from around the area. With more clients in the rural region, Blaise had been looking at his options. It made more sense for him to be living closer to them. He'd done the figures, thought about them for weeks, and when it appeared he wouldn't be able to see Dusty anytime soon, he finally made the decision. With the help of the internet and a friendly local real estate lady, he rented a modest home in Wilkton near the center of town. Another daring action, renting a place he'd never seen. But there were plenty of images on the internet site, and in the end, he was able to get a shorter lease agreement of three months, just in case it didn't work out. Or if it did, then maybe by then he'd be living on the farm.

Would I like living out there in the middle of nowhere? The thought knotted his stomach as he sealed the last box and scribbled 'Pots' on the top.

Based on how he'd been feeling without seeing Dusty, he reckoned he could live anywhere as long as she was there. She'd texted to say she was starting crutching tomorrow. Blaise was hoping to be settled enough to go and help her in the shed. He was determined to be there to give Dusty support.

"Stop looking goo-goo eyes and get moving, Blaise," said Scott as he came by carrying another box. "If you don't hurry up, you'll never get there."

"Okay, okay," said Blaise, and he picked up the last box in the kitchen. "Hold your horses."

"Well, you're sounding more country by the day. Maybe you were really born in the wrong area," said Simon as Blaise walked out to the truck.

Blaise laughed. Maybe he really was meant to live in the country.

DUSTY YELLED at the sheep to scare them into the shed ready for crutching. Ted barked in excitement, and the ewes pushed forward filling the shed. The shearers were inside setting up. James had come over to help her in the shed again.

What she really wished for was to see Blaise over the last month. She had missed him. A lot.

Dusty heard a vehicle coming down the driveway. *Who could that be?* But she didn't have time to stop to investigate. She closed the gate and walked through the shed, climbing over the fences weaving her way to the other side where the shearing took place. They would be starting soon.

The shearing shed door slid open. Dusty looked up to see who could be dropping by at this inopportune time.

Dusty's breath caught in her throat, and her pulse increased as Blaise stepped into the shed. He wore some Hard Yakka trousers and a matching working shirt. Dusty was surprised how much he looked at home in the shed. Not wearing a suit made a big difference, and he looked much sexier in his new work clothes.

"Am I late?" he asked.

"No. You're just in time."

"I've come to help." He paused. "That's if you need any."

"Are you sure?"

He walked toward her. "Yes. And I'm planning on staying."

"What do you mean you're planning on staying? Until the end of shearing?" Dusty's heart skipped a beat or two. There was something about the tone of his voice that suggested something much deeper was happening than Blaise merely coming here to help. She wanted him to stay longer than for the shearing, but would he move to the country? *Just for me?* Things had been going well in the last few months, but it was a big ask for him to uproot his life for her. And she couldn't move away from the farm. They hadn't talked about it. She was happy with their arrangement of seeing each other when they could, and for a long distance relationship things were going exceptionally well.

"Longer." He stepped up to Dusty and slipped his hands around her waist. "Much longer." He kissed her.

"Until the end of the month?"

Blaise smiled. "I've rented a place in town."

"You what?" This was more than she'd been hoping for.

"Well, you can't move to the city, so it made logical sense. I want our relationship to continue to grow." He brushed his fingers over her cheek. She shivered from his touch and from the excitement coursing through her. This was the next step of a serious relationship. And she was ready.

"I love you." The words came from his mouth in a soft breath that sent a bolt of heat through her.

Dusty kissed him.

They may have had a rocky start, but things were heading in a direction her heart had longed for—a loving, long-term relationship.

"I love you, too."

The End ~ for now

To be continued in
A Dusty Christmas

Enjoy more rural romances

By Lilliana Rose

The Royal Show Affair
A Farmer's Christmas

Best in Show
A Country Christmas

Like urban paranormal romance?
Check out these books by Lilliana Rose

Protector Wolf Shifter Series
Bk1: Shadow Wolf
Bk2: Marked Wolf
Bk3: Rogue Wolf

Dragon Bond
Dragon Reborn

Witch Moon Series
Bk1: Dark Moon Secrets

ACKNOWLEDGMENTS

Big thanks to my mom and dad, while no longer living, still provide me with the strength and inspiration to keep persisting and following my dreams. Thanks to my sisters who support their big sister in her writing dream.

Thanks to my friend, Marianne, who bravely read this novel even though it was out of her normal genre. Thanks to my friends who proudly bought this first novel when I was learning the craft of self-publishing.

Thank you, Kaylene for editing this novel so the love story between Dusty and Blaise can be shared with confidence.

ABOUT THE AUTHOR

Lilliana writes in contemporary romance. She grew up on a sheep farm in Australia, then swapped her work-books for city heels, and now lives in the city. She enjoys drawing on the contrast between country and city life in the contemporary romance she writes. For her moving to the city was like coming to a different country.

Check out more of her work at www.lillianarose.com
Connect with Lilliana Rose on social media.

www.ingramcontent.com/pod-product-compliance
Lightning Source LLC
Chambersburg PA
CBHW020605110726
47899CB00002B/377